Devon & Cornwall

Edited by Lynsey Hawkins

Disclaimer

Young Writers has maintained every effort to publish stories that will not cause offence.

Any stories, events or activities relating to individuals should be read as fictional pieces and not construed as real-life character portrayal.

YoungWriters

First published in Great Britain in 2004 by:
Young Writers
Remus House
Coltsfoot Drive
Peterborough
PE2 9JX
Telephone: 01733 890066
Website: www.youngwriters.co.uk

SB ISBN 1 84460 535 3

Foreword

Young Writers was established in 1991 and has been passionately devoted to the promotion of reading and writing in children and young adults ever since. The quest continues today. *Young Writers* remains as committed to engendering the fostering of burgeoning poetic and literary talent as ever.

This year, *Young Writers* are happy to present a dynamic and entertaining new selection of the best creative writing from a talented and diverse cross section of some of the most accomplished secondary school writers around. Entrants were presented with four inspirational and challenging themes.

'Myths And Legends' gave pupils the opportunity to adapt long-established tales from mythology (whether Greek, Roman, Arthurian or more conventional eg The Loch Ness Monster) to their own style.

'A Day In The Life Of . . .' offered pupils the chance to depict twenty-four hours in the lives of literally anyone they could imagine. A hugely imaginative wealth of entries were received encompassing days in the lives of everyone from the top media celebrities to historical figures like Henry VIII or a typical soldier from the First World War.

Finally 'Short Stories', in contrast, offered no limit other than the author's own imagination while 'Hold The Front Page' provided the ideal opportunity to challenge the entrants' journalistic skills asking them to provide a newspaper or magazine article on any subject of their choice.

That's Write! Devon & Cornwall is ultimately a collection we feel sure you will love, featuring as it does the work of the best young authors writing today. We hope you enjoy the work included and will continue to return to *That's Write! Devon & Cornwall* time and time again in the years to come.

Contents

The Creative Writing

Don't Be Ashamed, Be Proud

In the happy family bathroom of the Robinsons', Mr Toiletbrush cried and cried. The cleaning squad and Mr Toothbrush, his closest friend, started to get worried. They didn't like seeing their good friend so upset, so they asked him why he was so upset.

'I'm so ashamed. All of you have proper jobs. Mr Robinson would never go on without brushing his teeth and Mrs Robinson wouldn't be able to clean her house without you guys.' He pointed at the cleaning squad, then lowered his head. 'All I do is clean the toilet. No one really remembers me.'

'But that's not true at all!' The cleaning squad looked shocked. 'Without you the toilet would be filthy. They would be too ashamed to have their friends come over.'

Mr Toothbrush went over to Mr Toiletbrush and reassured him with a pat on the back. 'You are very important!'

The whole cleaning squad clapped and cheered.

From then on Mr Toiletbrush has always taken pride in what he does and never feels ashamed.

Marie-Janke Eloff (14)
Bramdean School, Devon

The Mysterious Burial

It was the 9th September 1834 and it had been three months since the last fatal murder in Texas. Three months ago saw the brutal and horrific murder of Mrs Stephanie Fullman in broad daylight.

She was approached from behind and stabbed several times in the head, by an ugly figure wearing black. She immediately fell to the floor and blood began pouring from her skull. Unfortunately, today we do not have any vital information about her killer. The only details we have is that he was tall and wearing a hat at the time of Mrs Fullman's death.

A week ago saw the private funeral of Mrs Fullman at St Augustine's Chapel. This was a very small and secluded place surrounded by many tall trees. The funeral was kept very secret and was only attended by her very close family. After the service, Mrs Fullman was buried in the small graveyard behind the church. She was left to rest in peace.

However, today her mother went to her grave to lay some flowers and when she arrived, she discovered that a small hole was appearing in the ground. Showing a feeling of disbelief, she ran away in terror. Suddenly, out of the ground appeared a rather bony figure, that of Mrs Stephanie Fullman.

Her mother was shocked to see the sight of her very beautiful daughter and ran back over towards the corpse. But then, just as she was approaching her, Mrs Fullman fell to the floor. Her mother knelt down to see if she had regained consciousness but there was no pulse. She was dead.

Jonny Telford (15)
Exeter School, Devon

The Third figure

Seldom does there occur such a happening so vivid, so powerful that it lingers in the memory forever. It was precisely this type of occurrence that I witnessed with my own eyes, a quite extraordinary event.

The night was young. I had been working nine strikes of the clock through six and I was in a state of utter exhaustion. Thrice had I been tired, so much so that I temporarily lost track of who I was. I retired to my chamber but, unable to calm my restless state, it entered my mind necessary to take a short, invigorating walk.

The first corner I had not yet reached, when a sharp piercing shrill broke the silence of the night. My head barely turned the corner when I saw two deeply shrouded men covered from head to toe in clothes of the night, barely visible in the beams of faint moonlight that lay ahead.

At this point, a third figure emerged from between the two. She (I concluded that she was a female upon hearing her scream) appeared in a great deal of pain. The masked men, I suspected still unaware of my presence, proceeded to perform the most gruesome of deeds.

One produced a sharp implement from his upper garment, whereupon he handed it to his colleague. The knife sliced through the air, slashing the skull from whence the dark life blood flowed freely. The fatal blow had been dealt and the body plummeted to the ground, where it lay still.

Tommy Purkis (15)
Exeter School, Devon

A Distant Aunt

(In the style of Edgar Allen Poe)

If my memory serves me straight, the entirety of my person was consumed in anticipation, as I looked past the foreboding black, rusting iron gates which separated the property from my senses.

Being no more than a hundred yards from the mass of grey, stone masonry beneath its black slate roof. I started to fancy what wonders could lie waiting for nature's rays to illuminate after a lifetime of darkness.

It was then that the solicitor appeared in my sight, emerging from the right hand side, striding down the dark, tree-lined gravel drive, carefully localising himself of my position.

We introduced ourselves, exchanged formal greetings and then he unlocked the gates. I followed through a garden choked with shrubs and brambles, towards the dark oak-studded front door of the house and he led the way down a poorly lit passage, panelled on either side with dark mahogany. The journey terminated in a most antiquated kitchen where I was duly invited to be seated at a large kitchen table.

The solicitor then positioned a large legal document before me and read from it, the details, culminating in a request for my signature upon the said document. I signed with good grace, for I was the beneficiary of the fine establishment I had just entered. It was left to me in the will of a distant aunt whom I had never met.

Later in the day, I recall sinking into a plush armchair at the side of the fire with my thoughts taking me down as many dark corridors in my mind as there were in the house. A deeply perplexing situation indeed.

Rob Hinds (15)
Exeter School, Devon

Story In The Style Of Poe

In the middle of the moonlit night, there was an ear-piercing screech that had obviously come from a female. It startled me because it was in the middle of the night. At first, I was motionless; the cause of the scream was puzzling me. I ran around the corner to find that people had already started to gather outside a door in the road.

I walked over swiftly to the crowd in the street. When I got there, I asked one of the individuals what had happened.

'Nobody knows what happened,' the old lady replied in a gruff whisper.

At the front of the crowd there was a group of men who were all demolishing the ancient door with axes!

After about two minutes, the men finally broke in. There was a great amount of people swarming through the door frame. When we got upstairs, there was nobody in the apartment. As I walked slowly around the candlelit room, I could not see anything unusual at first, but on my second time round, I noticed a bloody, still hand which was poking out of the curtain underneath the bed. When I saw this, I instantly dropped to my knees and lifted up the curtain. As I did this, I saw a pale face and wide eyes which were staring at me straight in the eyes. I quickly alerted the other people in the room. We pulled the corpse out from underneath the bed. This female had obviously been murdered because the bed covers were warm to the touch and had recently, been used also at the position of the body.

But the only mystery about this murder is, how the murderer had entered and escaped!

Chris Thomas (15)
Exeter School, Devon

The Castle Of Death

I waited. Huddled behind a large boulder. I could not see but could only hear, as the guard made his way past the boulder that hid me from his view.

His footsteps crunched against the dead leaves of the undergrowth and I listened as they faded into non-existence. I got up, careful to not even disturb a moth which had landed upon my arm. I moved slowly but assuredly, making my way up onto the edge of the trodden pathway. I persisted up the pathway, with only the moon stopping the total obscurity of the ground on which I traversed.

As I rounded a corner, I could make out the shadowy outline of the castle where I was headed.

As I neared it, it came into clearer vision and I could see the tall turrets and pointed towers through which I was supposed to navigate.

As I looked up at it, I was foolish enough to take my eyes off the ground. Not looking where I was going, I tripped on an obtruding tree root; my body falling down the side of a steep bank, which I now lay at the bottom of. I tried to stand up and immediately felt a sharp pain pulsate up my right leg. I limped towards the nearest tree and leaned heavily against it. I looked around, all I could see was the blackness of night.

Thomas Burchell (15)
Exeter School, Devon

A Day In The Life Of A Chair

'Oh comfy!' That was what they used to say every single day. But then they just took me away and put me in a cinema. The booming sound of romance, comedy and scary films, over and over again. I am old and knobbly now, according to every person, whether they are short or tall, dark-skinned or light, brown hair or blond.

Now I just sit waiting to be auctioned off, next to the old jugs, pots and pans and sofas. Stupid sofas showing off all the time, it is so unfair, I wish I was one (not personality-wise of course, always showing off about how they can hold more than one person - sometimes even three people).

They all take the mickey, just because I'm a boy with a flowery pattern as my cover. But I mean, so what? I don't care and why should anyone else care? Stupid upholsterers, stapling me with a new material, stupid, stupid, stupid! Everything is sooooo stupid.

'Going, going, gone! And this lovely old oak cinema chair is sold for £200.' That's not very much is it? Some sofas sold for more than £450.

But now I get to be in a museum. Everyone's looking at me (I feel so proud that people like the look of me). I have a little doll sitting on me, never complaining, ever.

I am so proud of myself! Nothing is stupid now. (Well maybe the upholsterer)!

Steph Taylor (11)
Ivybridge Community College, Devon

Cinderella

'Poor little Cinders!'
Mocked her ugly sisters,
As they prepared for the ball.
'Don't I look lovely?'
'Pah, you look ugly!'
Came the cries from the hall.

Back in the basement,
To Cinder's amazement,
A fairy appeared with a crown!
'Now dear,' she sighed,
'Just step aside
And I'll do what I can for a gown!'

'Now,' said the fairy
'Your head is all airy,
But this you must not forget
The magic wears off
At the chime of the clock
At midnight, back you must get!'

When Cinders arrived,
The ladies all cried,
Cos with Cinders the prince chose to dance.
She found it enthralling
The sisters were bawling
But then, what should happen by chance?

The clock started chiming,
Poor Cinders broke timing,
With whom she was dancing with now.
She rushed up the stairs,
Forgetting her airs
As the rags replaced her gown.

The prince went to follow,
His heart filled with sorrow,
As the one that he loved turned and fled.
She left a shoe,
The only clue,
By which the prince could be led!

He traipsed round the town,
Becoming more down
As each girl tried the shoe and sighed, 'No.'
But received such a shock
When an ugly old crock
Said that her sister might know!

The prince stepped inside,
And instantly cried
That this was the one it would be!
The foot fitted shoe
And the prince at once knew
That his bride would surely be she!

Hannah White (12)
Ivybridge Community College, Devon

Around The Bend

Suddenly, a big white van sped past me. It went so fast that it nearly made me fall over. Before I knew what I was doing, I had jumped to my feet and I was sprinting as fast as I could, to try and catch up with the van.

The van skidded to a halt! I hid behind the van, breathless from running. I watched anxiously as two women got out of the van. They started sprinting, so did I, they turned a bend, so did I.

I had just got around the corner when I heard a loud, piercing scream and to my horror, I saw a person being dragged through an open door. The door slammed shut behind them. *Bang!*

I was just about to go and see if the door was locked or not, when someone grabbed me from behind. They started dragging me somewhere! I had no idea what was happening or where I would end up, or even where I was.

Clang! I was hit on the head with a copper pipe . . .

Lorna Kirkby (11)
Ivybridge Community College, Devon

A Day In The Life Of My Dog Bonnie

I suddenly woke up from having the worst nightmare ever. It was about Maisy the cat, the chase was never-ending . . .

I'm not supposed to be here on this comfortable sofa, it's just my basket is so hard and smelly. So I creep onto the sofa and then creep back so that no one knows. I have to be quiet because the floor is so noisy. *Don't* tell the cats about me being fussy, they might forget who's the boss around here.

Paul the feeder has woken up and I sit here dying for some food. I wish he would hurry up (doesn't that toast just smell *so* good). God, I'm hungry! Now I need to do my business outside (if you know what I mean).

Then the boss and the 'pains' get up, can we go now?

We're now on site, time to change into 'watch out' mode. Mmm everything *smells* normal. Mmm everything seems quiet, *too* quiet!

A rabbit, go, go, go! . . . I missed it. Why are those sheep in my field?

'Bonnie, time to go home,' yells the feeder.

Home at last, I'm so tired. I think I'll waggle my tail to get my food. Yeah, this is the life lounging on the sofa. I need to be on my own . . . *No!* The 'pains' are coming, *Help!*

Click! The kettle has now boiled.

Saved by the bell, now I can get my biscuit dunked in coffee *yummy!* What a great day. Goodnight zzzzzzzz.

Georgina Baldwin (12)
Ivybridge Community College, Devon

War

Dear Znela,

I long to return home. Here I feel trapped in a constant snowstorm. Everywhere I turn I see destruction, hatred, anger and such evil.

With every step I unwillingly take, I sink deeper into the thick mass of loneliness, suffering and sadness. Wherever I reach out, I'm stung by the buzz of bitterness that hovers over everyone I touch. I struggle to see in this blizzard of conflict, everyone battling, arguing, fighting one another. Every face I see tells a story of misery. Each pair of eyes that meet mine are dark tunnels that have been emptied of all emotion or feeling.

Now their empty minds are hungry, longing for something to sink their teeth into. So the cruel takes advantage of the weak and those once innocent, free souls are fed on the evil that's so generously donated; leaking out of every crack in the Earth's surface. And once they've fallen victim to this monster, it becomes a drug, addictive and unstoppable. Snaking through their veins, poisoning their blood, coiling around their hearts, pulling tighter and tighter, suffocating their souls.

The captured visions of death and killing whipping around my head, make me feel dizzy. I stop, to my left I see a soldier returning home, he receives medals for how many lives he's taken, he's called a hero and is admired for his bravery.

Then I turn and I see two children, so frail and weak that they fall to the ground, with every step they take, gasping for breath. One of them looks up and what I see in those eyes can't be put down in words, but I know that amount of suffering should never be seen on any face, let alone a child's. They call out in pained, tear-choked voices. But no one will reply. They're all dead, strewn like litter, in-between the heaps of burning ash and rubble, that were once homes.

I feel, as though I'm drowning and the more I struggle, the harder it becomes. Until I'm just falling, faster and faster, deeper and deeper. Wrenched by the gravity at the fiery pit of this Earth's core. Like a stone that's been hurled down into a bottomless well.

Sheets of darkness slip past me. Every now and then I hear a whisper of laughter or catch a glimpse of happiness. I seize hold of these glimmers of hope, but they crumble to dust at my touch.

I search desperately for a way out, but I realise there is none on this planet, for these humans are controlled by one thing - *war!*

Yours, Knox

Karenza Fafoo (14)
Liskeard School & Community College, Cornwall

Panda-Monium In The Rainforest

(An extract)

She stumbled. That's when they got her, I remember that shot, it echoes through my head. It has haunted me ever since.

That shot killed my mother. I remember every detail of those men's faces (the poachers I mean) and I swore on my mum's grave that I would get revenge. I will, I know I will get them for what they've done. I'm going to train myself to kill. I have a few friends who will help me. There's Chwang the parrot, he'll help, he always does.

'No, no way! Come on, you're a panda, a six-month-old panda, just a panda!' squawked Chwang.

'Well I just . . .' murmured a defensive panda, 'I've just got to, otherwise my mum'll never rest in peace. I did swear on her grave and you're the one who's always lecturing me on you should never go back on your promises, blah, blah, blah this, blah, blah, blah that. You might as well help, I'm going to anyway, never mind what you say. I rely on yo-'

'Ssh, someone's coming. Hide now!' uttered the parrot. 'It sounds like a poacher. Don't move at all!' The leaves rustled up ahead. The tension was unbearable, it was truly terrifying. Around the little clump of bushes came a . . . *girl.* Well she didn't look so terrifying. Ju Sing was baffled, for he had never seen a girl before. He was totally bewildered. He edged out to her, ignoring Chwang's warning. He trusted his instincts and saw no threat.

Sally, for that was her name, stood stock-still. She had waited eighteen years for this moment.

Every time she saw a shooting star, she had wished. Every time she had blown out the candles on her birthday cake she had wished. There was her dream, standing right in front of her. She was amazed at how soft his fur was. How sharp his little black eyes were. Sally loved every inch of Ju Sing. She crouched down and they instantly bonded
Over the next month they built up their friendship; human and panda.

It was a strange friendship. Sally never let herself touch Ju Sing. Ju Sing did the same. Neither actually touching. That would break the rules of Mother Nature. But just because they weren't physically allowed to touch, mentally they were exploring each other. Sally was fascinated by Ju Sing and Ju Sing back again. It was the oddest of friendships and yet it worked.

Robyn Brewer (11)
Liskeard School & Community College, Cornwall

In The Alley

'Who's there?' bellowed Steve as he was edging his way through the dark, dull alley not knowing where it was leading to. He was using his hands, placing them on the cold, wet wall as he stepped out. He was walking as though he had a blindfold on. He heard someone's feet crunching on the gravel behind him. He spun around thinking someone was there but no one was. The hairs on the back of his neck were standing high off his skin.

He started to run but then he stumbled on a sharp object which pricked his skin but did not leave a mark. He sprang to his feet and was off before anyone could catch him.

He was jogging now. He ran straight into a wall and bounced backwards. It was like he had hit a trampoline.

He whipped his head around, thankfully seeing no one. He slid to the floor to rest for a minute. Steve heard the crunching of the feet again. He was looking around for somewhere to hide, then saw a large dustbin in the corner. He ran to it and crouched down and held his breath.

The figure moved into sight and stood, turning to look in every direction. Not daring to breathe, the creature was tilting his head to the side, like a predator looking for his prey.

He was now advancing towards the dustbin. Steve closed his eyes.

Adam Keenan (13)
Penryn College, Cornwall

Fateful Day

She ran. She had never been so scared in her entire life.

Tara Campbell, 14 years old, lived in a normal house with a normal family and had normal friends - until that fateful day when it happened.

It all started on a Sunday evening, she had just come home from her friend Naomi's house when she found her parents arguing in the front room about what colour to paint it. They had just moved house and were trying to get it all ready before her Aunt Sophie came to stay in August. It was already July, they had moved in three months ago and had only just decorated the kitchen, bathroom and Tara's parents' bedroom.

'Hello, I'm home!' yelled Tara.

'Oh hi sweetie! There's some toast in the toaster if you want it,' replied her mum.

'Okay, thanks!'

Tara went into the kitchen and walked to the toaster to get her toast. Suddenly, the arguing in the front room stopped.

'That's weird,' Tara said to herself.

She walked into the front room and screamed, her parents were hanging from the ceiling, a thin wire cutting into each of their necks. Tara could see the dark red bloodstains on their clothes. The blood was dripping down their necks, down their bodies and onto the floor. She could see the deep slits running round their necks.

Tara ran to the phone and listened, it was dead!

She ran out of the door and down the road, heavy footsteps following behind her . . .

Georgina Hopwood (13)
Penryn College, Cornwall

The Race Is On

'And they're off! Hulio II is in the lead, closely followed by Kirk, Spirit of Darkness III. Manes blazing as they all hurtle down the course but still at the start is Warlord VI.

Warlord VI is the newest and youngest competitor this year - but back to the race. Oh my God, Warlord VI is catching up. The black sheep in this race is catching up to the group.

We are now seeing the most amazing race this year. This is the first time a racer has caught up from so far behind. This is amazing, the horse has caught up and is chasing the leader, Hulio II. What a race!

This new racer is giving the leader, Hulio II, a run for his money and he has overtaken. Warlord VI is the new leader. He has overtaken the whole group and is winning.

They're getting close to the finish, it's going to be a photo finish Hulio II and Warlord VI are head to head and they've finished. We will have to wait for the photo to find the winner - I have now got it! The winner is . . . *Warlord VI.'*

Jessica Oakes (13)
Penryn College, Cornwall

Late!

I push the heavy doors; I use all my strength to push it.

All I see when I walk through the doors is the last late pupils and a long hallway which never ends. I have to go to the office, I try to ask someone where to go but they just ignore me as usual. It was probably the other turning I had to go in. I always make mistakes like that, I never think. That's why I never fit in. I was always chosen last. Always picked on. I thought this school was going to be different, but no it's exactly the same.

At last the office, at least one good thing happened to me today. It's no good hoping I'll fit in because I'll always be a misfit. So now I've got to look for room twenty-two. It's nine o'clock and I'm already fifteen minutes late, my first day as well! My feet echo on the walls along with my heart thumping.

Sweat starts to form on my head as I walk up to the door. I check the number with my timetable; it's definitely the right room;

Room 22
Mrs Dillwater
Science

I start to get panicky. It's going to be exactly the same, except this time I'm going to get beaten to death. My feet echo loudly, getting louder and louder, faster and faster. I push the heavy door which seems so light.

I run away from the school and my life.

Charlee Tresidder (13)
Penryn College, Cornwall

Running The Gauntlet

Every morning, fear takes a-hold of me; I presume you're wondering why? It is because of the four-legged beasts that live at the end of my lane.

Let me explain; I'm not afraid of dogs, I actually own dogs but these are no ordinary dogs. These will attack unprovoked. Every day I wait until the last minute to walk to my bus stop and face those beasts.

First I start down the lane, fear trickling down my cold, sweaty spine. I think to myself, *come on Tim, just go one step at a time and they won't hear you,* but they always hear me.

I creep closer, this could be my lucky day. I start to jog. Yes, I'm clear. But I hear a low snarling behind me, I know they're here. I break out into a run, I can hear them coming closer, I turn round as one of the beasts launches itself into the air . . .

Tim Churchley (13)
Penryn College, Cornwall

Cross Channel Ferry

There is a creak then a bang as the door swings, then falls off its hinges. The smashing of the bottles as they fall from the shelves. This is the worst trip I have ever been on. I feel sick as the boat rocks backwards and forwards, I want to be somewhere else.

Only two hours ago I was on land in Plymouth, I should've got out of the car then and said, 'Have a nice trip, see you when you get back!' But no, I didn't! Now I'm about three hours from France. I wish I could fall asleep and dream of being home in my bed, instead I'm stuck here sitting in an uncomfortable chair, listening to the sound of strangers vomiting. Lovely isn't it? I think I'll go to the bathroom.

Loads of people are sitting around looking grumpy because they can't sleep either. I pass the perfume shop on the way and most of the bottles have smashed now. I feel sorry for the cleaners. I'm in the bathroom and urgh, it smells bad. I've got to get out of here!

Only an hour left, then it's on solid ground. Ah, that thought makes me happy. Then the announcement; 'Ladies and gentlemen, we will be arriving in Roscoff shortly, we hope you enjoyed your trip.' Yeah right! A lot of happy customers today! Better get back and find Dad.

And here we are in France at last. Solid, dry ground. I hope the trip home isn't as bad!

Hayley Tonkin (13)
Penryn College, Cornwall

The Witch Of Dunston Village

A long, long time ago in the quiet and sleepy village of Dunston, there lived an old lady in a nice cosy cottage, at the edge of the village. Everybody thought that the old lady was a witch.

One day a young boy called Isaac went out to play. He got to the village green where he saw a fluffy white rabbit. Isaac chased the rabbit to try and catch it but he lost the rabbit's trail. After a couple of minutes, Isaac found the rabbit and he noticed that it had a cut on its paw. Isaac went to catch it to look at its foot but the rabbit kept on running.

Isaac followed its blood trail to the cottage door where the old lady lived. He knocked on the door and the door opened. He went inside to find the old lady bathing her foot where she had cut it. He asked her whether she had a rabbit and the old lady replied by saying, 'No!' and that she never had.

Thomas Hosking (12)
Ridgeway School, Devon

Headless Horseman

This ghostly rider has been seen in different forms all around the world, made popular by 'The Legend of Sleepy Hollow', written by Washington Irving.

Legend says that a man hired by the British Army in 1776 to help in a revolutionary war, died a most horrific death. His head was taken off by a cannonball. According to legend the now headless horseman returned in a ghoulish form, taking heads from the living and depositing them in Sleepy Hollow, New York.

The Story Of Jonathan Storm

September, ten years ago, location Crane Street. Jonathan Storm was in for a case of bad luck.

After studying long and hard for a career test, he gave up and decided to go to his girlfriend's house. It was a cold, dark, blustery night but he decided to walk to Kathryn's house. A fateful decision, he should have driven! The breeze would clear his mind for the forthcoming maths test.

Not aware that he was being followed, Jonathan turned the corner into Reneman Lane. A dark rider on a pitch-black stallion swinging a blade as sharp as King Arthur's came galloping along beside him.

Jonathan seeing the rider, broke into a sweaty panic, he ran like never before. He was so close to Kathryn's house, in the confusion he ran into Douglas Park, forgetting there was no way out. He realised that he was trapped.

Horrifically, the last thing he saw was the glimmer of a blade. Jonathan was found the next day, outstretched at the gates of Sleepy Hollow cemetery.

Patrick Stuart (12)
Ridgeway School, Devon

The Legend Of The Necro Dragon

Once, many millions of years ago, there was a small town afoot a jet-black mountain. This mountain was inhabited by a dragon known as the Necro Dragon because of his black scales and flame.

The Necro Dragon tormented the town, destroying homes, eating crops, animals and people. Many warriors had tried to defeat the dragon but none had prevailed. Until one day, a wizard and his travelling companion entered the town.

For one reason or another, nobody seemed to give them any hospitality. They went to see the town leader and the wizard told him of his vast power and that he was going to vanquish the Necro Dragon. The town leader allowed them to go up the mountain to defeat the dragon.

So the wizard and his companion hiked to the top and used the tunnel to travel to the dragon's lair. Unfortunately, the dragon had sensed their presence and was ready. He blew and a jet of pitch-black flame emitted from his mouth. The wizard summoned a shield to protect himself. He then used a water spell but dragons are impervious to magic. The companion revealed himself as the legendary Knight of Nedleg.

It was a long battle to the death, each side taking and dealing blows. Neither side was willing to give up, until the dragon with a mighty swish of his tail, killed the wizard. This made the knight furious, so while the dragon was distracted with the wizard he seized the opportunity and (using his mighty blade) caused a weak part of the cave to collapse, crushing the dragon and saving the town.

After this, the knight settled down in the town but he never forgot his friend, the wizard.

Luke O'Connor (11)
Ridgeway School, Devon

Haunted Trip

I was alone, everyone else had a roommate. The place appeared haunted. Mr Barber, my school teacher was in the room next door. My sister Jade and her friend Kerry were in the other. I had a small iron bed with a thin white sheet.

We stayed in this place for a week and two days. The first night I could not sleep, I heard noises, noises I was not familiar with. I went into Jade's room, the door was locked, they were asleep.

What should I have done? Finally, I decided to go to Mr Barber and tell him I was scared and that I needed a roommate. He did not listen, he ignored me.

There I was, lying on the bed reading a book which my father had given me, when I heard a scream. I didn't know what it was. I shouted for Jade and Kerry, they didn't hear me. What was happening? It began to rain hard, soon there was a storm.

A few nights passed, I wanted to go home. I thought to myself, *there are only two more nights in this haunted place.* I searched the house, it was deserted, I thought to myself, *tomorrow is my last night in this place.* The day seemed ages, then the final night. Creepy as ever, alone again!

I fell asleep in an old chair that was beside the bed. The night passed quickly and I packed my bags early in the morning. Home I went and here I am now.

I have told my short story of my school trip to you. It was fun to tell, imagine if you were in my situation. What would you have done?

Jessica Suggett (12)
Ridgeway School, Devon

The Teddy Escapes

'It was a fine day, the sun was shining and everything was normal. Although someone was plotting a scheme.

In a bedroom far away lived Ted, the small furry teddy bear. Ted had been planning this for weeks. Today was the day Ted escaped!'

'Tell us more Grandpa, tell us more!'

'Okay Son,' replied Grandpa Ted. 'Ted ran for the door. He looked around, checking for danger. Then he crept like a lion, ready to pounce slowly to the other side of the hall and hid. He looked down to see the stairs, a cliff dangerous to all teddy bears. This bear was about to go where no bear had gone before!'

'What happens next Grandpa?'

'Be quiet and I'll tell you . . .

Ted jumped a stair, he fell to his knees. Then he hopped down the next stair. Suddenly he saw the banister. He climbed up as fast as he could, then he reached the top triumphant, but that wasn't the end. He had to think fast, the frightened teddy bear fell on his bum and slid down, getting faster as he went. He shut his eyes and out of the blue, he hit the bottom with a thud.'

'Did he die Grandpa?'

'No, he didn't let's see what happens next . . .

He jumped down when the cat saw him. He was a giant who wanted his prey. He ran frantically around the house then he leapt for the cat flap. Jubilantly he walked away and saw the dog! This dog ate poor Ted the teddy bear.'

'On no Grandpa!'

Joshua Barwick (11)
Ridgeway School, Devon

Jade And Jodie, The Best Subject Of The Week

Jade and Jodie were best friends, they had been best friends since Year 1. They did everything together, they both went to Green's School, they both had Miss Ball as a tutor, she was fun.

As they went to their first lesson, English, Jade and Jodie talked. Jade loved English, Jodie hated it. Jodie was always daydreaming, but Jade always had her hand up.

When Mr Jeff asked Jodie a question Jodie didn't know what to say, Jade, in the end, answered it. She always answered them. These were the worst lessons of the week. At the end of the lesson, Mr Jeff asked to see Jodie, Jade waited outside.

Mr Jeff said that Jodie may have to move down a group because she never answered any questions.

When Jodie told Jade, she was horrified. Jade hugged her and said, 'Everything will be alright.'

Jodie told her mum, she said it was her own fault for not paying attention. Jade said that Jodie had to get better. So every night Jodie went to Jade's house and they studied all night long.

Jodie started to pay attention in class and English became her best subject. Mr Jeff was amazed, he had never seen such an improvement. Jade loved English more because Jodie loved it too.

They started to win medals, they even represented England in a writing competition. Jodie was so proud. Her life was great because she still had Jade as a friend and it was all down to Jade.

'Jade the great' she was called by Jodie.

Gemma Collings (12)
Ridgeway School, Devon

Dolphin Talk

'Would you like chips for tea?' Karen asked.

Lilly nodded and beamed with delight. It was Lilly's birthday and she was looking forward to opening the card her mum gave her. It was a wonderful glittery envelope, but the anticipation got the better of her and she ran over to the envelope and ripped the paper. A card with flowers on was in Lilly's hands.

She opened the card and out fell a pair of tickets to swim with dolphins! Lilly ran into the kitchen and gave her mum a huge squeeze. Karen saw the tickets in Lilly's hand and realised what the hug was for.

They soon ate their chips and went to bed. Lilly couldn't sleep, she was bursting with excitement, dolphins were her favourite animal and she couldn't wait until the next day.

Karen plaited Lilly's hair and they set off to the Marine Wildlife Park.

They got changed into some wetsuits and plunged into some water with a beautiful waterfall and tropical plants.

An instructor came along and introduced herself. 'Hi guys, I'm Lucy and you must be Lilly.'

Karen looked at Lilly and smiled.

'I'll bring in Bubble.' Lucy put her fingers to her mouth and made a high-pitched squeak. In swam a playful young dolphin. Lilly was smiling. Bubbles and Lilly played all day, swimming and diving, playing games and doing tricks.

The day soon ended. 'Thank you Mum, it's been the best day of my life.'

Karen looked at Lilly. 'You just spoke!' whispered Karen in astonishment.

'It's the dolphin, I need you to know how happy I am!'

Jade Leeke (12)
Ridgeway School, Devon

A Kidnapper's Evening

'Let me go,' screamed Iahde.

'Shut up,' shouted Mike, as he hit her. She screamed, and he cut her leg with a knife. 'Do that again and you'll be dead!' *Ring, ring,* 'Hello, I have your daughter, listen!' he rammed the phone into Iahde's face and she screamed for help.

She sat there while he arranged for her mother to drop £100,000 to the other kidnapper, Joe. The drop was to be made at the Halliday Café at seven-thirty tomorrow morning and they would let her go at twelve.

She was suddenly picked up and shoved into a bleak, disturbing room, it was totally empty, not even a window. Joe and Mike walked out, loudly locking the door. She got up, she had to get out. Mike had told her mum she would be killed if the police were told about this. *She can't pay,* thought Iahde, *we are poor anyway.*

She went over to the image of a door and pushed. It actually opened with a loud clang, she braced herself, but neither Joe nor Mike heard it. The door opened out to the outside of the building, Iahde climbed down and ran. She ran and ran and ran until she almost collapsed.

She eventually found a payphone, dialled and reversed the charges. Her mum answered, 'Hello.'

'Mum, oh Mum, help me. I got away from them. I'm in a supermarket in Wetfield Place, please come and get me.

'I'm on my way,' replied her mum.

'Okay, bye Mum.' She ran into the shop and minutes later her mum arrived and she went home.

Eleanor Davies (11)
Ridgeway School, Devon

Money Man

It was about a week ago. There was a scream in the village and I went to investigate what was going on. I stepped through the door of the house and there in front of me was a woman on the floor, dead. It was Mrs Barwick, an old woman, in fact my next-door neighbour. Her face was pale like a ghost. I noticed her mouth was half full of money. It had been the second murder that week. The other victim had been killed using the same technique. I suspected they had been suffocated.

I heard a door slam. I jumped in shock thinking that it might be Money Man. I ran to the back door, opened it, with the power of a mighty giant. It looked as if it could be Money Man scrambling over the fence. I ran like a lion trying to catch my prey. I only just managed to get over the fence. I was a few paces away from him when I fell on my ankle. It was broken. Money Man stopped and ran towards me with a treacherous look on his face. Like a bat from deep, dark depths of Hell.

In utter shock I noticed a sharply pointed dagger in his left hand. He plunged forward trying to stab me. Luckily I was able to roll over. Money Man fell and I noticed something peculiar, Money Man was in fact a woman. She had died from the shock. When she was taken for forensics, it turned out that she wasn't the killer . . .

Samuel Wright (12)
Ridgeway School, Devon

The Fourth Dimension

There was a young girl who always had homework and only a small amount of playing time. Her name was Bella, she had long brown hair and piercing black eyes. She was still in school, she was eighteen years old. Her favourite thing to do was play on the computer.

Bella's favourite game was The Sims. She was crazy about it - she ate, drank and slept The Sims. She was playing the game once and obviously she was playing with her Sim equivalent, when she heard a funny noise. It was a rumbling noise that was getting louder.

She felt a sucking wind pulling her to the computer and as quick as a flash, she was somewhere else. She was in a small house all alone, until she heard a small noise and then a sudden bark.

'Who are you?' Bella asked.

'Where are you?'

'Help me, now!'

A dog peered from the corner of the bush. Bella went over to him and a woman came and said: 'There you are Luna, I don't want you around this house anymore. Oh, I'm sorry my name is Claire Charming, are you the tenant?'

'No I'm not, I'm Bella.'

'Why?'

'I don't know where I am.'

'You are in The Sims.'

'Wow!'

'If you're not careful, I'll turn you into a toad.'

'Please don't.'

'Relax, chill, stay cool.'

Bella stayed and told Claire all about where she came from and what it was like. Meanwhile, Luna slept . . .

Samantha Foort (12)
Ridgeway School, Devon

Tigger's True Love

'Tigger it's time for your nap,' said Tigger's owner Paige. Paige cuddled Tigger into her arms and headed to his hutch.

What does she know, I just had the best day ever. I was out doing my day job when, (I'm quite embarrassed) I saw a female rabbit munching on some nearby grass. She was very beautiful. The bad side of it was I had lost my job. The reason was I made a racoon love a bird.

I really wanted to talk to her but I became really shy. What you don't know is I've got a plan to escape. There's a bunny party tonight and I think she'll be there.

(Tigger kicked his hutch door open and hopped away. The campfire was just about to start. There were lots there.)

I stopped in my path. In front of me was the beautiful rabbit. I just stood and stared.

'Hi, are you going to the party?' asked the beautiful female rabbit.

My mouth went dry and I was speechless.

'My name is Storm, I am the head love maker's daughter.'

'I, uh, think you are beautiful,' Tigger stuttered. 'We'd better hurry, we don't want to be late,' Tigger said, catching his breath.

'I guess so,' replied Storm.

We hopped away towards where the campfire was. Storm and me spent the whole party chatting and telling jokes to each other. I couldn't believe the time we spent together, it was such fun.

I was given my job back. *The best day ever!*

Paige Murphy (12)
Ridgeway School, Devon

The Hand In The Hedge

On a hot summer's day, Jake was at Ernesettle golf course with his mate Ryan. Ryan was trying to teach Jake to play golf, seeing as this was Jake's first attempt (he hadn't been doing very well at all). Ryan, however, had been playing golf for six years.

Ryan took his shot. *Whoosh!* 'That's the way ya wanna hit it, Jake!' exclaimed Ryan proudly.

'Wow! My turn, my turn!' screeched Jake in an excited voice. He eyed up the flag of the sixth hole, with great anticipation. He lifted the club right up to his left ear. He heaved it down with great force. The ball glided through the air. It would have been an amazing shot, if he was aiming for the hedge in the middle of the course. *Plop!* The ball landed smack in the middle of the hedge.

'Way ta go, hot shot!' Ryan said sarcastically.

Jake ran down to the hedge to look for his Topflite golf ball (it was his only one). He was just about to give up looking when he saw something shiny amongst the shadows. He hurried closer to it. It was then he realised it was a gold ring on a hand sticking out of the ground. Jake didn't know what to do, he was stunned. He had never seen anything like this before. In fear he crouched to pick up the golden ring. The hand clenched into a fist and grabbed his finger.

'Aaagggggggghhh!' Within an instant, he was gone.

Lance Jobe (12)
Ridgeway School, Devon

Meddling Music

Arriving at my music lesson I couldn't help noticing it was extremely quiet. Opening the door I was horrified to find my music teacher impaled on a music stand. There was blood on the ceiling and the walls, there was even blood seeping into the carpet. I checked his pulse rate. It was non-existent. He was dead. I ran out to the next room but the teacher was bound and knocked out.

I looked at my phone. 'No battery,' I said to myself. What should I do? I decided to run, run to the front office to get help. Panting, I explained the whole thing to the secretary. Amazingly she didn't believe me. So I made her follow me to the scene of the crime.

When I opened the door she went cross-eyed before fainting. How was I supposed to know she fainted at the sight of blood? I needed to get to a phone so I ran back to the front office and phoned the police.

The police tracked the killer down using fingerprints they found on the music stand. They tracked him to 1 Saw Street, where they discovered it was the victim's next-door neighbour, who had killed him for practising music too loud.

The neighbour was sentenced to ten years, imprisonment for manslaughter. As part of his rehabilitation, the killer was forced to learn the piano.

Paul Rogers (11)
Ridgeway School, Devon

The Battle Of The Freaky Zone

Me, called George Hunt, and my friends Nick Lanser and Carwood Imprus were just three more soldiers lost in the middle of World War II.

We were in the middle of a forest which was very cold and was always snowy. It was all very quiet until bombs started dropping and trees exploded around us. We just jumped down and took cover - we were vulnerable.

After the bombing was over I asked, 'Everyone OK?'

'Yeah,' replied Nick

We carried on walking, being more cautious this time, hoping there were no more bombs. About thirteen minutes later, we stopped and stared. We looked at three German soldiers dropping their weapons.

'What the . . . ?' I said. Then I saw something really freaky, I nearly fainted. Three German tanks came up behind the soldiers and we were too shocked and scared to run.

The three German men smiled and waved but then they turned around. They walked up to the tanks, stuck their heads in and next we saw a couple of heads on their way to Japan. I was amazed. Then, to make things even more weird, the tank drivers got out of the tanks, bowed and started kicking each other's butts.

All Nick could ever say was, 'Yeah.'

'OK,' I said.

'Yeah.'

'Let's go now,' I said.

'Yeah.'

'Right,' I said.

'Yeah.'

'Will you shut up with the yeahs!' shouted Carwood.

'Yeah.'

'Come on, let's go and leave the freaky zone now,' I said.

'If we're leaving the freaky zone we've got to leave Nick as well, he is really annoying me,' said Carwood.

'OK, goodbye freaky place,' I said.

Mark Povey (12)
Ridgeway School, Devon

A Day In The Life Of The Queen

Today is a very important day for Her Majesty. This morning I got out her best clothes and then went to awaken her. She was in a surprisingly good mood. Her morning tea was brought in, afterwards she got into the bath I had prepared for her.

When Her Majesty had bathed she called to me and I dressed her in her finest clothes and then followed her down to the dining room where she had breakfast alone as Prince Philip was away on a royal visit.

At about eleven o'clock we had a state visit from the President of the United States of America, with him he brought twenty men. He was staying at the palace with the Queen. He had a brief talk with Her Majesty before they had a light lunch consisting of duck paté with Scottish oat cakes, fresh salmon with seasonal salad and a last course of fresh fruit meringue. Spring water was served throughout the meal.

They then had a longer meeting about current world affairs before going to their bedchambers to change for a state banquet later in the evening.

At about four o'clock I began to help Her Majesty to dress in an imported silk gown with a diamond necklace and earrings and a very elegant diamond and pearl tiara.

The banquet consisted of five courses. For starters there was caviar, chicken liver paté and a bottle of Shiraz Australian wine, then a North Sea mixed fish dish with a light rosé wine. The main course consisted of roast pheasant, roast lamb and a Chateau Frederic followed by sticky toffee pudding and custard and to finish, cheeses of the Commonwealth with the finest port.

The Queen had the Prime Minister and other important people with her. The evening ended with everyone saying goodnight and going to bed.

I dressed the Queen in her nightgown and bade her goodnight. I then prepared Her Majesty's clothes for the following day before retiring to my own bed.

Caroline Bell (12)
Ridgeway School, Devon

Just My Luck

Hi, my name is Jodie O'Connell and I love to go down to the park. I always go down the park with my friends, Kirsty Pocock and Sally Gibson.

One day, when it was Friday the thirteenth, the three of us went down the park, not realising it was a bad luck day. When we started to mess around in the playground it started to rain. As soon as we took shelter it stopped. Then when I ran up the steps to go down the slide I fell over and landed in a puddle. As Sally and Kirsty were laughing their heads off at me, I quickly ran to the swings.

When I was sitting on the swings, Sally came running over to push me. As Sally was doing so, the swing broke and I fell right on my bum. It had kind of hurt as well. So after the problems I had had, I decided to go to the Ridgeway.

Sally and Kirsty came along with me and I had to go first didn't I, knowing me. I had another problem, I had stepped in dog's muck. Then when I was getting the muck off in the river, my shoes got soaked as Sally pushed me in.

We finally got there when we walked past a huge crane. Just in time as well because the crane toppled over just as the three of us walked past it - just my luck!

Jodie O'Connell (12)
Ridgeway School, Devon

Sherlock Bonez And Daxter, His Faithful Companion

'We're on the case.'

'What case? What case?' Daxter asked Bonez anxiously.

'This missing fish case,' Bonez replied, not having any hope for his companion, Daxter.

Sherlock Bonez is a detective in dog form. He is nothing without his trilby and sunglasses. Along with his faithful companion (yeah right) Daxter, they can solve any crime (nearly). Daxter is a ginger, stripy beaver who walks on two legs along with Bonez.

Whilst searching for clues, Bonez noticed a shadow lurking in the bins in Tommygun Alley. Bonez went to investigate.

'Wait uuup . . . ouch.'

'Ssshhh!' Bonez urged.

'Hey the bin was in the way!'

As they carried on they came across a fishy smell.

'Something fishy's going on. Ha, get it? Fishy!'

Daxter saw the look on Bonez's face and said, 'OK, no, it wasn't that funny.'

Suddenly a cat jumped over the cobbled wall onto the slabs hissing a deafening screech.

'A-ha!'

'What?' Daxter shouted.

'A-ha!' Bonez replied.

'Shut up!'

Silence.

'That's better. Now, what were you saying?' Daxter casually walked over to a funny-shaped bin bag and sat on it.

'He's the culprit!' Bonez said in amazement.

'Uhhh, who?' Daxter looked around in puzzlement. By the time he had faced back, Bonez was tugging at something beneath him. Daxter jumped up. 'Argh, it's a cat.'

'Yes, he's called Scrabbles and you nearly killed him.'

'Well how was I to know it was a cat?'

'Oh well you saved the day.'

'Wowee!'

So that's how it was. It wasn't Bonez who saved the day, it was Daxter. It proves that miracles do happen!

Tamsin Trollope (12)
Ridgeway School, Devon

I Think I'll Just

I was free, they didn't chase me, even at walking pace, so I ran. I was soon out of the gates and making my way to *the alley* as planned. I turned the corner. Suddenly something hit me in the face. I screamed then I realised who it was. 'What are you doing here? We arranged to meet in the back alley.'

'Ya, I know but I was just like so excited I never thought we would see the day when you, *Chari,* became one of the gang.' Max grinned at me I tried not to meet his eyes. What I saw was much worse than Max's filthy face, my eyes were led down a midnight-black alleyway infested with creatures.

'I think I'll just . . .' Max interrupted me before I had time to finish my sentence, 'run!' he gasped, his voice sounding worried. What on earth could be the matter? Max darted round the corner and licked his lips. I looked at the smidgen of chicken on the top of a dustbin.

'Dinner is served,' Max said, chewing on the vile platter which you could hardly call dinner.

'I think I'll just . . .'

'What?' said Max, interrupting yet again and with that I was off out of that disgusting, filthy place.

I made my way home to be tucked up into a nice, warm, cosy bed. I gave out a huff and said to myself, 'I suppose my master was right saying never to mix with back street dogs. I now know what a filthy, horrible, unexciting life they lead.'

Rebecca Talbot (12)
Ridgeway School, Devon

The Heist

He stormed into the bank holding his pistol at the ready. 'Hold it right there! Nobody move!' said the robber, pointing his gun at one of the cashiers who had a horrified look across her face.

There was a loud crash as another masked robber leapt through a window and grabbed a cashier and directed a pistol to the back of his head. Both robbers stood fixated in their black, skin-tight suits, motionless and masked. One of the robbers was short and stocky and the other was tall and lean.

The first thief jammed the door with a fire extinguisher and pulled the floor to ceiling window blinds down whilst the other kept an eye on the cashiers.

'Empty the tills!' demanded the second thief.

The cashiers followed the demands obediently and handed everything to them. Then in the office behind a phone rang.

The first thief went to investigate it. He wandered out slowly and cautiously. He thought it would stop but no, the phone just kept ringing so the robber kept walking. He turned into the room and searched it with his gun. He saw the phone and drew it from its holster. 'Hello,' said the robber in an innocent voice.

The voice at the other end of the phone was one of a woman's and was quite high-pitched. The voice asked, 'Hi, is Sue there?'

The robber answered the person in his innocent voice and said, 'No. I think you've got the wrong number,' and then he hung up.

Meanwhile, back at the cashier's desk the cashier ran under the blind and smashed through the window. The second robber shot at him hopelessly but he escaped.

Everything froze. Then on the screen it said 'Game over!'

Jack Philpotts (11)
Ridgeway School, Devon

Nan's

It was a horrible day.

'Ben wake up, it's time to go to your nan's,' said Ben's mum.

'Uhh, I don't want to go to my nan's. It's so boring, she only lets me go out until six and she feeds me turnip and she always makes me do the dishes,' Ben said.

'Get in the car Ben, or I'll drag you there and ask your nan to feed you extra turnip!' said Ben's mum.

'Oh okay, I'm coming,' said Ben.

Several minutes later:

'Okay Nan?' said Ben.

'Alright Mum?' said Ben's mum.

'Yeah, okay my little sugarplum Ben?' said Ben's nan.

'Okay, I'm going to go now, bye Ben,' said Ben's mum.

'Bye Mum,' Ben said as his mum left.

'Right, I think you can start on the dishes then you can hoover up the whole house and then you can clean up the garden. Be careful there is lots of dog poo from Jake,' Ben's nan said.

Two hours later:

'Ben, dinner,' said Nan

'Yuck, turnip, I hate turnip!' said Ben. 'Can I go out after dinner please?'

'Not until you have done the dishes,' said Nan.

'Okay, right where are the dishes?' said Ben.

'Right here,' said Nan with a huge pile of dishes beside her.

'Nan, I've done the dishes,' said Ben.

'Okay, you can go out now until a quarter past six.'

'Yippee!' shouted Ben in joy.

Bang! Bang! Bang!

'Oh my ankle, I rode over a ditch,' said Ben while he was crying, *'Nan!'*

'What, what's wrong Ben?' said Mum.

'I just had a horrible dream,' said Ben.

'Okay, calm down, you're going to your nan's in a minute,' said Mum.

'What? *No! Argh!'* said Ben.

Then it *really* happened!

Ben Clark (11)
Ridgeway School, Devon

Raiders Kings Again

On Sunday 28th March 2004, the basketball match at the Plymouth Pavilions was the Plymouth Raiders against the Bath Romans.

At the start, Gavin Love, the co-captain of the team, was practising and warming up with the rest of his teammates. Gary Stronach, the team's coach, was talking to the refs about how seats were filling up quickly. Foxy, the mascot, was trying to get Mrs Foxy to attend their very tense match with a full house.

During the match Gavin scored nine points, made three steals, tried to score five three-pointers but scored none and had five free-throws but scored three. He also got substituted once. During the time-outs and breaks, Foxy danced to the 'Shake Your Tail Feathers' song and did his trick twice. His trick is he runs up to a trampoline, jumps on it and tries to make a slam-dunk. He made it once.

At the end of Sunday's match the score was 97-53 to the Raiders and because they won the trophy they put on their number one T-shirts to celebrate. At the beginning of the award ceremony the co-captains, Gavin Love and Dean Williams, lifted the team's EBL trophy to show they had won it and also got awarded with their medals.

Gavin Love said that he enjoyed the match and was pleased, honoured and excited when lifting the trophy.

Gary Stronach said that he was pleased with his team and enjoyed the celebrations.

So after their tense match with a full house and with a successful win they enjoyed their well-deserved celebrations and medals.

Nicholas Horton (12)
Ridgeway School, Devon

Black And White

Joey had been travelling through dense forest for three days. He set out from his uncle's house after being told about Thorn, the lady of black magic. Joey's uncle gave him a sword and he had also said it was a magical sword of white magic.

Joey was at the entrance of Thorn's lair but he was still wondering what magic the sword had. He guessed it was white magic because his uncle had said it was a war of black and white magic and as Thorn was a black magic user it was pretty obvious.

He entered Thorn's lair. He was in a hallway, it was dark and it reeked with black magic. There was only one door at the other end of the hallway. Joey went to this door.

Joey opened the door into a room. At the back sat Thorn, the lady of black magic. Joey drew his sword. It shone white in his hands. Thorn screeched when she saw this and jumped up. She drew her sword and it shone purple and she asked him who had sent him. Joey told her about his uncle and she laughed and said, 'That old man's got someone to try and kill me. Hey well once I'm done with you I'll go and finish him off as well.'

They ran at each other and fought for two hours. Joey delivered a hard blow and Thorn's blade shattered Joey's sword then went straight through Thorn's heart and the war was over. White magic had won.

Stephen West (12)
Ridgeway School, Devon

Birds And Ice

As the eagle gracefully flew round the mountainside, Jadane the white archer, whistled for the eagle and without a thought, the eagle plunged down to meet its master on the side of Mount Talky in a small cave.

'Elwer the most beautiful and loyal of animals,' the elf said softly, stroking the elegant creature.

The lord of birds crouched for his master to climb on his giant back. The eagle's wings were steadily balanced in the light wind, his feathers durable in the breeze. You'd think they were as hard as rock. Then they swooped down the mountainside only to be skimming the tops of trees.

Seconds later, they'd both seen a sudden darkness and a flush of black flame followed by a shot of ice in the opposite direction. The elf quickly steered the eagle round the mountain and had seen Seperoth the witch lord of Duruthrein hunting the most mythical of beasts, Ice Phoenix from the legendary ice caverns.

They made haste and parked in front of the dark lord and his black dragon. Jadane pulled out his bow, whipped out an arrow from his quiver and shot a thunder arrow through the shadow dragon's wings. Its sharp jaws made its screams echo through the land. The witch master healed his black dragon quickly.

'You stupid fool of an elf, spare your life for this mythical creature or die with it!' he shouted in anger.

Before long the Ice Phoenix had fled and was out of sight quickly. The witch lord drew out his staff in anger and started chanting the same words over and before the archer had time to react, the witch man's black oak staff sent dark shadow venom vines shooting at Jadane. The eagle however, quickly glided to the side, lucky enough to dodge the venom snakes of shadow.

Straight after, Jadane jumped to his feet and directed the eagle down and steered it up behind the witch and shot a flame arrow at the dark rider.

Seperoth's scream of death was deafening. It sent all animals scurrying away from their nests. All around felt its evilness. The ex-lord of Duruthrein fell off his beast to his death.

Jadane glared as he fell then dived down and glided west in search of the white warrior, Dundin, for council of the Ice Phoenix.

Jack Weldon (12)
Ridgeway School, Devon

Valentine Crush

One day Aimee was waiting for a special card, because it was Valentine's Day. She waited for about an hour and finally the post came. There was one there for her; she was so excited about getting a card. Aimee was a bit embarrassed about opening her card in front of her mum. She slowly opened the card; it was so beautiful. She looked inside. The verse said, 'Please be my Valentine 'cause I love u!' But the thing was she didn't know who it was from.

The writing that was in the card, she had never seen before. Aimee was hoping it would be from her school crush Duncan. She went upstairs crying and thinking about all the times she had asked him out and the answer was always a big fat *'No!'* Aimee cleared her tears and thought it might have been Duncan who had sent it, but he didn't want her to know.

In the middle of her dramatic moment she got interrupted by her mum.

She said, 'Someone's on the phone for you, dear.' Mum passed her the phone.

'Hi Duncan what's up?' she said.

'Nothing really, just thought I'd ring up and see if you'd got your card,' he whispered.

'Uh yeah, was it from you?' Aimee said clumsily.

'Yeah it was, I hope you like it. Well I have to go now, see ya,' he said.

So for the rest of the day Aimee was smiling.

Emma Glanville (12)
Ridgeway School, Devon

School Crush

It was just another normal morning at school. Chloe, Micky, Emma, Chloe and me were just stood in the playground having a deep discussion about a prior night out on the town. The bell rang and rudely interrupted us. As my friends and I strolled to class, Matt leaned over to me and said, 'Alright Jade, are you playing football today?'

My heart melted as if I was sat on a burning fire. I slowly replied, 'Yeah sure but don't kick me in the shins today!'

He went off laughing with all his friends.

I finally got to class and sat in my normal spot. I sat at quite a grotty table in the corner of the classroom. I was sat down reading my favourite book in the corner, *Megan.* I was so into it that I wasn't even listening to what the teacher said. Then all I heard the teacher say was, 'I'm going to move a few of you round today!'

I've never liked moving seats because I always end up sitting next to people I don't like.

Everyone had moved seats except for five people - me, Michael, Micky, Chloe and *Matt!* I heard my name being called by the teacher (I was dreading this part) and then the second name was read out, *'Matt'* I couldn't believe it but there was one problem, my best friend Micky was going out with him. Did I not tell you that?

We had just finished maths when the bell rang for break. Micky and all my friends were yelling at me, saying, 'Why were you flirting with my boyfriend?'

I ignored her and walked off. Fancying a boy who's girlfriend is your best mate isn't called *school crush* it's more like *dead crush!*

Jade Herring (12)
Ridgeway School, Devon

The Escape?

Long ago in Alcatraz prison three men were talking.

'When I get out of here I'm going to murder the little snitch who dobbed on me,' Vince chuckled.

'I'm gonna join the Mafia,' said Marco.

'I'm going to start a new life not committing any crimes,' I said.

'Let's go!' Vince chuckled.

Marco pulled out a home-made bar spreader and spread the bars of our cell. We ran round the corner and hid in a cupboard.

'A guard!' Marco whispered.

'Hang on!' I whispered back. There was a thud. I clubbed him in the head, he slumped to the floor in a heap. Vince picked up his weapon and we carried on.

We ran to the courtyard door, it was our only escape. Marco pulled out a rusty silver key and put it in the keyhole. We heard a lock close, I swore, an alarm sounded and I swore again. Vince loaded the gun and laughed loudly. A guard came round the corner and was shot and he fell to the floor. Four more guards came round, this time they shot Marco in the arm before they were killed.

Another guard came round, threw a gas bomb and was killed. Unfortunately it wiped out Vince and Marco.

I was the only one alive. I picked up Vince's gun and tried to protect myself. I was useless with a gun - I was better with a knife. I was captured and taken to the courts, I was sentenced to death.

Robert Ashton (11)
Ridgeway School, Devon

The Animal Prison

Betty the chicken was in a cell with Shamus the dog and Bubbles the mastermind cat.

'Remember how we all got in here, this pig of a prison?' Betty said sadly.

'Are, are you taking . . . oink, oink . . . the mick Betty?'

'No, of course not!'

'I think you are,' Shamus said.

'I'm not taking the mick out of Oinky.'

'I believe you Betty, now let me tell you how I got here,' said Bubbles.

'It all started when I needed to go for a number two, so I found the nearest building, which was Jordy Library, so I did my business in there. But then this man started to chase me, he jumped and caught me with his net. The next thing I knew I was in here with you lot.'

'I'll tell you how I got here,' said Shamus the dopey dog, 'I felt tired so I thought I'd cross this road and fall asleep on the bench. I got halfway across the road and must have dropped down asleep. The next thing I know I'm in this dump with Betty.'

'So I think it's my turn. Well anyway here we go . . . I, Betty Booty, was doing a protest campaign against Animal Prison so I decided to sit in the middle of the A38 and refused to move. But then a white thing pulled up and a man got out and grabbed me then dumped me in here,' said Betty in a sad voice.

'When will someone come and take us as pets!' said Betty Booty, Shamus the dopey dog and mastermind Bubbles.

Jacob Vincent (12)
Ridgeway School, Devon

How The Leopard Got Its Spots

Many years ago leopards did not have black spots they were just plain, golden carnivores.

It was a scorching day in the savannah. The leopard was crouched low, blending into the grass. He had spotted some prey, it was a herd of zebras crossing the plains right in front of him. The leopard ran out, bit the zebra on the leg. The zebra straight away fell on the floor. The rest of the herd just ran away. The leopard ripped the zebra into pieces.

The leopard had been munching on the zebra for a good two hours. While the leopard was ripping through the zebra, the beautiful sunny day turned into an horrific night storm. This storm consisted of thunder, lightning, black clouds and really heavy, torrential rain.

The leopard immediately stopped munching and headed straight for the forest. The rain was pouring on him, he was very frightened of both thunder and lightning.

He was running as fast as he could until finally the leopard had reached the forest. The leopard sat down under a tree which created a lot of shelter for him. Then, without warning, the leopard was hit by the rain. It started creating little black spots.

Finally the storm had gone. The leopard walked out from under the tree. The leopard was still golden but with black spots all over his body; and that's why the leopard now has black spots and not just plain, golden fur.

Steven Tall (11)
Ridgeway School, Devon

Hercules

Long ago, powerful gods lived on Mount Olympus in ancient Greece, ruled by Zeus.

Zeus and his wife, Hera, had a baby boy. 'I shall name him Hercules,' exclaimed Zeus.

Hades was jealous of Zeus, because he wanted to rule Olympus. Hades was determined that Hercules would not get in his way.

Meanwhile, Hades, thinking Hercules was gone, proceeded with his conquest of Olympus. Hercules grew up to be a helpful man.

'Only gods can live on Olympus,' Zeus said. Zeus told Hercules to seek the help of Philoctetes - trainer of heroes.

Days passed by. Hercules slowly mastered all the hero's skills. One day, Hercules said to Phil, 'I am ready to fight real monsters.'

Phil replied, 'Okay, we will go to the city of Thebes.'

So they set off to the city of Thebes on Pegasus.

Hercules reached the great city of Thebes. Hercules cut off the Hydra's head but more heads appeared in its place. By using skills Phil had taught him, Hercules eventually defeated the creature. Little did Hercules know that all the monsters had been sent by Hades to destroy him.

The same night as Hercules was training, Hades paid him a visit. He brought a young woman, Megara, with him. Hades promised that if Megara was harmed, Hercules would get his strength back. Hades quickly unleashed the tornado, rock, ice and lava Titans - evil monsters that had incredible powers.

Hercules was battered without his god-like powers. Megara had fetched Phil. When they got there Phil encouraged Hercules to fight on.

With renewed hope, Hercules attacked the Cyclops with a burning stick. Megara was hurt. She persuaded Hercules to stop Hades attacking Olympus. When Hercules and Pegasus got there a colossal battle was fought, during this Hercules got his strength back. Hercules had saved Olympus.

Thomas Willis (12)
Ridgeway School, Devon

Swen News

It doesn't make sense.

Girl of thirteen has amazing senses!

Jessica Lea earlier revealed in an exclusive interview all about her incredible power!

Jessica, who lives in Germany, revealed that she has an incredible extra sense! Believe it or not, she has actual *X-ray vision!*

Psychologists have done many tests and have all agreed that it's no fluke!

Psychologist Angela Crimes says: 'I've never seen anything like it before! It beats all explanation!'

Nothing like this has ever been recorded before! In the interview Jessica said: 'I never told anyone about my gift, because I was afraid of being teased. But now everyone knows and people were a bit wary of me at first, especially at school, asking me what they had for breakfast and things like that. But now everyone's fine about it!' No one really knows how she got this power, but Jessica has unusually large pupils.

Jessica Lea later told us: 'It's great having a special gift! It makes you stand out. When other people found out, we had loads of people coming to our house, asking me if they had cancer and things. At first it scared me, but then my mum started charging a small amount of money for me to see them, because we are not rich and we needed the money. It soon became great fun and it was wonderful to tell a woman she was going to have a baby! But it was awful to tell someone they were very ill'.

This is an amazing story that I'm sure none of us will forget! Jessica is a truly amazing child!

Danielle Spring (12)
Ridgeway School, Devon

How The Tiger Got His Stripes

While the tiger was at home thinking about his future, a zebra passed by. The tiger said, 'Gee I wish I could have stripes like that zebra.' He wished and wished.

One day he went for a stroll in the park and he passed a zebra and that zebra was in fact a very artistic zebra; they both stopped and the tiger explained to the zebra that he wanted stripes like him and the zebra agreed.

That particular night, he decided to go to the swamp to cool off. To his surprise his stripes came off with ease.

The next day he bumped into the same zebra and the zebra said, 'My stripes obviously didn't work then.'

But as they walked their separate ways their tails got tangled up and the zebra's stripes on his tail fell off and landed on the tiger. The tiger looked like he had seen a ghost. Ha, ha, ha!

Hannah Baggott (12)
Ridgeway School, Devon

A Day In The Life Of My Mum

'Sarah can you empty the dishwasher for me please?' I stood near cooking dinner.

'Oh! But Mum I really want to go outside!'

I just looked at my daughter, wishing she could help me out quickly around the kitchen. We had important guests coming over. I gave a small smile. 'Go on then, remember though dinner won't be long. Be back about six o'clock!' I knew she'd be back late because she never listens to anything I say.

'I'm really sorry everyone. I haven't a clue where Sarah is, she should have been back an hour ago. I've tried ringing her but she isn't answering.' I then heard the front door slam. 'Sarah!' I got up off my seat and went to find Sarah covered in mud from head to toe, with ripped trousers and a ripped top. She couldn't stop giggling.

'Sarah!' I tried to keep my voice down as it was very embarrassing in front of my new boss. 'You are such a mess, go clean yourself off, you're an hour late!'

Sarah just rolled her eyes.

Ring! Ring!

I woke up and realised it was just a dream; I was my mum and dealing with the situation that we had yesterday. I answered the phone.

'Hi Sarah, do you want to come out?'

'Sure I'll just tell my mum.' I ran out to the garden.

'Mum . . .'

'Sarah do you think you could help me hang up the washing, it's a big job.'

'Well actually . . .' I saw Mum struggling and decided that instead of being a pain in the neck, *I would help.*

Alice Royle (12)
Ridgeway School, Devon

A Day In The Life Of A Pencil

When I was an immense, powerful tree, hundreds of years ago, along came *them!* The woodcutters as I now know since attending school. They severed, slashed, sliced and hacked me. I once had great dreams of becoming a coffee table or even a chair for someone special to sit on, but *oh no,* the humiliation of it all; I was to become a laughing stock, as my life as a pencil began, in the grubby hands of a filthy child and his mucky pencil case.

Each day as I come out of the dark of his pencil case, I get sharpened by his best mate, Sharpener. Minute by minute I become teeny-weeny and undersized.

Here we go again, he's bored so in the mouth I go. Maximum dribble, saliva side to side, moving around slowly like a slug. Then I'm left to dangle on those rocks, which he calls teeth.

Clatter, clatter as my rubber head is yanked off and spat across the room, spinning towards the teacher. *Whack!* It's landed slap bang on her arm.

Across the room she comes, pulls me from his mouth and slams me on the table at 30 miles an hour. Gigantic teeth marks all down one side that join other previous scars. Every time he puts me into the jaws of death, I cry silently, 'Stop,' but for him to hear my cries of woe it is like getting blood out of a stone.

The teacher's words of 'Don't keep putting that pencil in your mouth,' fall on deaf ears as I am left doomed to face the same fate over again in what is to be my short life.

Now the day is over and the grimy boy returns to put me back in the deep, black hole, the pencil case. But wait, someone else has picked me up, a dark-haired boy with glasses. Maybe, just maybe, tomorrow will be a better day.

Tom Morgan (11)
Ridgeway School, Devon

A Dream Of Kings

Rupert was a very solitary boy who only had one slightly crazy friend who didn't laugh at him. The reason for this is because over the years he had played the most horrendous practical jokes on people and he had lost all the mates he had. But he didn't play any on Rupert because Rupert was so down in the dumps all the time (from being laughed at) that nobody would laugh not even Jonnie Havelock, the nastiest boy in class. Rupert was, as I said, very solitary and lonely until one stormy night something unexpected happened. . .

Rupert was turning in his bed. It was the most horrible dream - Paddy and Jonnie had pulled down his pants and everybody was laughing and then suddenly everything went gold. He was in a palace and he was sitting on some kind of throne. Out of the pits of his stomach came an almighty grumble.

'Thou oust hungry,' Rupert ordered.

A servant came rushing up. 'I can get yee ribs sire,' and then it dawned on King Rupert he was the king in some fairy tale.

As Rupert ate he watched a jester making himself look stupid for money. He gazed at the jester and thought, *if only I was a king.*

Ring, ring, ring! Rupert woke up suddenly. Everything was gold

'I'm hungry,' Rupert said, without looking at anything.

'Yes sire.'

Was it a dream or not? I'll let you decide.

Joe O'Hara Childs (12)
Ridgeway School, Devon

It's Behind You

It was a beautiful Saturday evening when Adam found himself stuck in doing his homework after a brilliant match of football.

Adam had short blond hair that made him look as though he was a celebrity; he also had light blue eyes that twinkled in the light. His teeth were as white and straight as they could be. All in all, good-looking.

Later that night when everyone was asleep, Adam slipped out into the darkness and into the moonlit streets, where all you could hear was the wind. Now and then a cat would scavenge around the dustbins.

Adam finally reached his destination. The place was an old, battered, broken castle that was once used in a battle.

He entered the castle cautiously. As he went in he saw a huge set of stairs in front of him that had cobwebs and spiders hanging from them. All he could think about were the horror movies he had watched when most of the people would enter and something would happen to them.

He was now in the castle and a sudden shiver crawled recklessly down his back. He dare not move. All he could do was move his eyes. No one was there next to Adam, yet he didn't feel lonely. He felt as if someone was beside him. He turned round and only saw the door.

Adam moved slowly towards the stairs when something came out from behind him and . . .

Kimberley Barber (12)
Ridgeway School, Devon

Tapestry's New Home

It was early in the morning when Tapestry awoke. She lay in the stable thinking about the day ahead and the children who she would be giving rides to and how long it would be until she couldn't give rides anymore. Oh how she would miss it, giving rides to laughing children and the nice cool sea after a long day's work.

She was interrupted by Fred (the stable boy) as he woke her friend Star and fed Star and Tapestry with carrots and other vegetables.

Tapestry got up and stretched her legs, it was almost 8 o'clock and the beach was already filling up. Tapestry wandered out of the stable and across the sand towards Sam, her owner and greeted him. Already there was a queue of children wanting a ride so Tapestry went to her place and felt someone being lifted onto her back and heard the girl laugh as Tapestry walked in the soft, white sand.

At the end of the day she heard Fred and Sam talking about sending Tapestry to a sanctuary. Tapestry was upset about leaving the stables but also quite excited.

Next morning a trailer appeared and Tapestry walked into the trailer. The ride to the sanctuary was very bumpy and as they pulled up to the sanctuary she felt nervous. When she walked into the donkey pen she saw loads and loads of other donkeys and children. Never once did she feel nervous or worried and she also was the favourite donkey with the children.

Rebecca Middleton (12)
Ridgeway School, Devon

The Girl Who Met The Racoons!

Once upon a time there was a young girl named Angelina. She was a beautiful girl who lived with her grandfather near a big, dark wood.

One day Angelina's grandfather asked her to go into the woods to find the big apple tree and collect some apples. Angelina dressed up warm as it was getting rather cold outside. She picked up her straw basket and set out for the woods.

Angelina saw the big apple tree not far in front of her; she began to run to the tree as she couldn't wait to taste one of the juicy red apples.

Angelina passed a pine tree. She stopped in front of the tree and she saw a group of racoons talking to each other. She tiptoed closer and she actually heard human voices coming out of the racoons' mouths.

One of the racoons turned around and asked Angelina, 'Are you here for apples?'

Angelina replied, 'Yes.'

The racoon walked with Angelina over to the apple tree. He collected some apples off the tree and handed them to Angelina. She put the apples into her basket and suddenly all of the racoons ran back to the pine tree and climbed up it.

Angelina ran home to her grandfather. He asked her what took her so long. Angelina told him about the racoons and her grandfather didn't believe her.

The next day Angelina went back to the woods. The racoons were nowhere to be seen! From then on Angelina would go to the woods and search for the racoons!

Elena Calley (11)
Ridgeway School, Devon

Ducklina The Duckling

One glorious morning in the middle of July, a little duckling wandered out of the pond. The duckling was called Ducklina and she lived with her brothers and sisters in the pond.

Ducklina was a good duckling and loved to explore in the rushes nearby. Although she was small she was nimble on her feet and the fastest duckling in her family. She was nearly past the gate when she felt the ground move and fell over. She thought it was an evil earthworm that was going to eat her alive.

Ducklina saw a big plastic thing and went to hide in it as she thought it would be a good shelter. But she was wrong. A human came up, grabbed the bag and it was then that Ducklina realised that the whole thing was just a trap. Ducklina was terrified; she had never been so silly in her entire life.

The journey was long and poor Ducklina was so tired, she fell asleep in the bag. She had a dream that she was on a boat in the harbour and she was swimming in a bowl of fresh, cold water. She awoke with a jump and found, to her surprise, that she was actually swimming in a bowl of water. Ducklina looked up into the human's eyes and struggled to get to the edge of the bowl as quick as she could, but as soon as the human saw her flapping, she grabbed Ducklina and cuddled her close.

Soon after this encounter, Ducklina and the human became friends and played together.

Ducklina was very happy indeed and she lived happily ever after.

Leanne Savage (12)
Ridgeway School, Devon

Coldest Day Ever!

Today the coldest ever temperature in Britain was recorded. In London people woke up to find their houses covered in snow and they could see frost and ice for metres around. The lowest temperature known was minus thirty-one degrees centigrade, it was recorded just outside of Edinburgh.

Many shops, offices and schools were closed because their staff could not get to work as their houses were snowed in. The roads were slippery and the gritters had been out since six o'clock this morning.

BBC weather forecaster, Louise Smith, said, 'It has been the coldest day for many years in Britain and I expect that there won't be another day like it for a long time'.

Most people decided not to brave the cold and stayed inside by the fire. Those that did dare to go out wore lots of layers, hats, scarves, gloves and almost all of their clothes! Hospitals were full of people that had been injured in car crashes because of the ice on the roads.

In hilly areas such as Dartmoor, people made toboggans out of metal trays and slid their way down to the bottom of the hills. It is fun while it is here but it is getting warmer and the snow will soon melt.

A warning is being given by weather forecasters everywhere to remind people that ice is dangerous but if you do choose to go out, wrap up warm and don't stay out for too long.

Lucy Saunders (11)
Ridgeway School, Devon

Messages

One hot day in the north of Canada, there was a pop group called 'Alive'. In the group there were four girls and two boys. The girls' names were Kelly, Hannah, Samantha and Amy and the boys' names were Daniel and Joe.

One day Hannah and Amy decided to do some cleaning. They started upstairs in Daniel's room where they found a piece of paper with a message on it saying, 'Meet me in the club'.

'Who is this from?' Hannah asked Amy.

'Don't ask me,' Amy replied.

'Daniel!' they shouted.

Amy and Hannah ran down the stairs.

'Daniel did you write this?' Amy asked him.

'No.'

Hannah put the message in the drawer and tried to forget about it.

The next day Samantha found one saying, 'At seven o'clock'. She put that one in the drawer with the other one.

Over the next couple of days each member of 'Alive' found a message. On 9th April the group put all six messages together. By doing this they made a complete note. The note said, 'Meet me in the club at seven o'clock on Friday, 11th April. Sing 'I Will Miss You' and I will be at the back of the club. Come and see me after the song'.

So that was what the band did. They sang 'I Will Miss You' and when they finished they went to the back. It was Kyle, an ex-member of the band and he wanted to know if he could be in the band again. So they became 'Alive' once again.

Kirsty Pocock (11)
Ridgeway School, Devon

The Chase

Jimmy and Ali walked into their bedrooms and got changed ready for the mission.

'Ready?'

'Yep, let's go,' said Jimmy in a foghorn-like voice.

They followed Lance downstairs into the underground and into a secret doorway behind a big poster of Jackie Chan that led them to a humungous underground garage which had all sorts of cars like the Ferarri F50, some Jaguars, some BMWs and a couple of Porsches but there were many more cars.

'Now let's go.' Ali revved up the engine and went at the speed of light to get to their destination.

By now Ali and Jimmy were in a nearby car park and were on their way to the front of the Prime Minister's house.

'Do you know what the plan is?' asked Ali. In an instant Ali got out his tranquilliser and shot the security officers and they slept like babies. 'I'll go after the money and the Prime Minister.'

'Alright let's go on the count of three. One, two, three, go!' encouraged Jimmy.

Back at their house, Lance was having a cup of tea with his good old friend Roger. Roger . . . ummm, well Roger his friend.

Back at the Prime Minister's house, Jimmy and Ali were on the landing trying to find the safe room.

'Stay behind me and look out for anything,' whispered Ali.

At the end of the hallway there was a big door that must have been the safe room.

Detective Lyspie was hot on their tails watching every move they made. Ali went up to the door and gave it a knock.

'Who's there?'

There was silence then Ali and Jimmy broke in, gabbed the Prime Minister, got the money and ran.

Steven Brooks (12)
Ridgeway School, Devon

A Day In The Life Of A Tiger

I awoke and slowly opened my eyes. I could see the beautiful bright sun rising up over the treetops. There wasn't a cloud in sight. The sky was a wonderful blue; with the occasional light breeze brushing through my fur.

I stretched my arms forward as far as they would go and then clawed into the ground. Bringing my back feet forward to get up, I turned around and saw my little cub. He was rolling around on the floor, enjoying the sunshine. I put my paw against his face and ran into the bushes.

As I got to the other side I pounced into the long grass and looked up. I saw two vultures flying above me. They had dark grey feathers and big vicious beaks. I was staying low; waiting for the exact right moment to pounce.

Eventually, one of them came down low. I jumped up for it but it swerved past me and flew away as fast as it could. This alerted the other vulture to my presence. It sped towards me, its sharp beak in line with my face. In the blink of an eye, I dodged the attack and clawed it down to the ground. It was clearly dead. I grabbed the vulture in my mouth and went back to my cub.

I couldn't see him anywhere. I ran to the tree where he was playing before and dropped the vulture. I roared out loud. Some leaves fell on me from the tree. To my relief, my little cub was there. He ran down the tree and we ate the food which I had caught and then went to sleep at sundown.

Ethan Lott (11)
Ridgeway School, Devon

My Day In The Life Of Jonny Wilkinson

The birds were singing in the trees, a light breeze was in the air and the sun was glimmering through the clouds. I got out of bed feeling different. I went downstairs and had breakfast. I opened the kitchen curtains. Blinding lights were flashing through the windows, it was cameras. I sprinted up the stairs with a shock. I had hairy arms and legs, and then took a look down my pants and I liked what I saw!

When I arrived at my bedroom I looked in my wardrobe but none of the clothes were my new size. I snuck into my daddy's bedroom and took a look in his closet. I grabbed a pair of his old flares and a checked shirt. Once changed I got my hair gel, then I realised I was *Jonny Wilkinson.* I had undergone a change into one of the greatest rugby stars in the world!

I went outside and was surrounded by a swarm of reporters and fans. In my pocket I felt my daddy's car keys. I jumped into the car and started the engine. I drove away knocking over several people. Before I knew it I was on the run from the police. It was thrilling and frightening, with all the turning and swerving. Eventually I lost them, and hid out in a pub. I had a couple of drinks, and then I got kicked out. I made my way home. Then things went hazy. The next thing I knew I was in hospital with an injured shoulder. I had a guilty conscience. Not only had I put several people in hospital, I had also injured England's perfect ten. I had learnt a valuable lesson from this - always to be me!

Brantley Rogers (12)
Ridgeway School, Devon

Stuck In The 1900s

My name is Jack. I'm thirteen years old with blond hair and blue eyes. I live with my mum who worries a lot. I'm going to tell you about the experience I had when I was nine, which made my life change. I went back in time!

It was a cold autumn night. I was in my warm cosy bed in my small house. It was in the middle of a thunderstorm. Rain was pouring down and a gigantic boom sent shivers down my spine. I got up and tiptoed into the hall. Making my way through the silent house, I opened the door of the bathroom. Then there was another bang which sent me hurtling towards the bath! The next thing I knew I was falling down towards nothingness.

When I woke up, I was in a weird deserted village. I pinched myself thinking I was in a dream but I wouldn't wake up.

Suddenly I was aware I wasn't alone. A small girl around the same age as me was cautiously walking up to me. She was a pretty girl who said her name was Zoe. She had shy blue eyes and ginger hair. The strange thing about her was, whilst I was wearing jeans and a sweater, she was wearing a long brown dress and a clean white apron!

I asked Zoe why she was dressed up and where everyone was. She said that everyone was out and that the clothes she wore were the clothes everyone wore in the 1900s. When she said that my heart froze. I had gone back in time and only Zoe could help me get back home!

Hannah Kennelly (11)
Ridgeway School, Devon

A Wand Is Pink And Silver

Many years ago Cinderella was mopping the floor of her basement when a fairy approached her. In a surprising manner Cinderella jumped and said, 'Get out of here now, I don't want you getting the floor dirty, and what is that liquid dripping from the end of your wand? It looks like cake icing to me and it tastes like it too,' as a drop landed in her mouth.

'I'm sorry Miss but my wand landed in the icing on the stove upstairs and I was only able to get it back out because the wand caught the piece of silver ribbon when it fell. I'm ever so sorry but the ribbon has formed a star and got stuck to the end of my wand. I sure do love my new wand.'

Cinderella looked very funny because she didn't know whether to laugh or cry The energy running through her veins was unbearable and she suddenly blurted out, 'Your wand looks beautiful, I wish every wand was like that.'

Although Cinderella knew that she would have to do the icing again, she knew she had done a good deed, and, from that day onwards, every wand was pink with a silver star melted on the end.

Dean Smith
Ridgeway School, Devon

Why Tigers Have Their Stripes

One day a plain orange tiger was playing in his own field and was having a laugh. He was thirsty as he had been playing and it was extremely hot. The tiger was drinking out of the water trough, when out of nowhere came a zebra. The zebra, out of the corner of his eye, saw the tiger looking at him and immediately stopped drinking. The tiger was not at all happy with the zebra because he had come into the tiger's field and drank his water.

The tiger started attacking the helpless zebra and the zebra fought back. As the tiger was angry, he was really putting a lot of effort into fighting the zebra. They had been fighting for a long time and they were both very tired so they stopped fighting. As it was hot, the zebra was sweating, he decided to get another drink while the tiger was not looking, but the tiger saw him and went over.

As the zebra was tired, he fainted and fell on the tiger. As the tiger was moving around trying to get the zebra off him, the zebra's stripes rubbed off and went onto the tiger, so they both had black zebra stripes. The stripes came off because the zebra was sweating and that is how the tiger got its stripes.

Emma Lister (12)
Ridgeway School, Devon

The Big Race

It was the day before the Grand National and all of us were getting ready for the big day. It was me, Devon Loch, and my best friend, Storm Wild and we were having some fun for the last time before the race. Storm has got a pure white coat with long, silky, braided hair and we've been best friends all our lives.

The next day had come, today was the day of the big race. I was really confident that I was going to win but last night Storm asked me if I'd let him win because he'd never won a race before. I'd always beaten him but I was just concentrating on the race. We were walking around in the pen and every time I looked around, I would see Storm looking at me, as if he depended on me to save his life, but I was not going to let his owner, the Queen Mother, down.

We went back in to have some food before the race - I was really starting to feel the pressure now and not just on the race, on the friendship between me and Storm. Is it Storm that's being selfish or is it me? In just those few seconds I had to make one of the hardest decisions of my life. The race was just about to begin, the adrenaline was rushing; this was it, the real thing. Then the gun had been shot, we were away and I was running like I had never run before. I didn't stop, the crowd were going wild, and we were coming to the end. I had the lead - just a few more steps and I was there. Then I thought about what Storm said. I fell straight to the floor. Storm had won.

I may not have won the race but I have won my friend.

Jamie Wigg (12)
Ridgeway School, Devon

How The Leopard Got His Spots

Long ago there lived a leopard and an Ethiopian man. There also lived a zebra and a giraffe. They all lived together in a place called The High Veldt. All the animals were a yellowy-brown colour. The leopard and Ethiopian would hide behind rocks and would scare the passing zebra and giraffe.

After a long time, the zebra and giraffe learned not to go to those parts of the High Veldt. They decided to look for somewhere else to live. They went to the forest; it was a lot different from their previous home, it was full of spots, stripes and blotches.

They hid in the shade of trees, safe and sound.

Meanwhile the leopard and Ethiopian were getting hungry so they asked Baviaan, a wise monkey, where they went. He said they had gone to the forest. So off they went.

In the forest the zebra and giraffe had changed. The zebra had black stripes and the giraffe had brown blotches.

The leopard and man had been in the forest for days searching for the other animals when they finally saw them near the trees. They saw a big difference. Then the leopard asked what had happened to them. They showed them how they could hide very well. The leopard and Ethiopian were so fascinated they decided to change themselves too.

The Ethiopian went a black colour and the leopard had some brown spots.

That's how the leopard got spots.

Alex Bird (12)
Ridgeway School, Devon

The Girl With A Golden Tail

Once upon a time there was a beautiful girl who lived in the sea. She had a shimmering tail that swished through the silky sand.

Diving through the waves was how she spent her days. It wasn't always like this though! She used to live with her father who was king of a wonderful country. When she was a one-year-old, she was snatched from her cradle by an evil witch from the sea. The witch was jealous of the tiny child so she cast a spell that would give her a tail and take away her legs.

Her father was devastated. He desperately searched for a brave man to break this cruel spell but even the finest soldiers could not face the evil witch. When they saw her many octopus legs and twisting grey hair, and not to mention her deadly red eyes, they cowardly ran away.

It was helpless until a poor village boy decided to take on the witch. With no fear at all, he said to her, 'You are an amazing witch!'

'I know, but now you must die.'

'But before you kill me, can you show me how you turn into a fierce lion?'

Immediately she turned herself into a lion.

'I bet you couldn't turn yourself into something as small as a slug though,' he said cunningly.

As soon as she turned herself into a slug, he jumped on her and squashed her to the ground. People clapped and cheered. The little boy had won the king's daughter back and broken the spell. He was rewarded by travelling the world for as long as he wished. After this they all lived happily ever after.

Hannah Stamp (11)
Ridgeway School, Devon

The Scared, The Pain

Hi I am Charlie and I am a dog, a very badly treated dog and my owner is very mean to me.

There was this one time when Mike, my owner, was on the drink as always. He then shouted my name. I knew what I had coming so I ran and hid behind the sofa. I hoped that he wouldn't notice me behind there. I then tucked my head in-between my paws. I felt the sofa get pulled back and my mouth suddenly went dry. He dropped his hairy arm around my neck and picked me up by my scruff. He had a big, brown stick in his hand which he then threw at me.

'Ow!' I yelped. I then managed to free myself and ran out the front door which Mike had left open when he came home. I then stayed on the streets for a night.

In the morning a family picked me up and now I am happy with them. I shall call it 'spoilt rotten'.

Abby Cock (12)
St Ives School, Cornwall

Wish Upon A Star

One day there was a girl called Sabrina walking in the park. She was about to go on the swing when she felt an *'ow'*. The *'ow'* was a star shining on her face.

'What is your wish?' questioned the star.

'Cool! A talking star,' said amazed Sabrina.

Sabrina wished to be a fairy, and the wish came true. She had purple, red and orange wings. She told her friends all about it. One of her friends called Kimberly knew a wish poem.

Sabrina set off home. She had a routine in the afternoon. She gets a cup of tea (one dessert spoon of sugar), she has a bath (with scented candles), has her dinner (cheeseburger), feeds her cats (Puss-Puss and Pip), rings her mates and then goes to bed and reads for half an hour.

Next morning Sabrina woke up with a flash! She saw an envelope on the floor. Inside she found some money and 2 tickets to see Busted (VIP area to meet them). 'Oh my goodness,' shouted Sabrina.

Suddenly she remembered the star and wished for the concert to be tonight. *Bing-bong!* She and Kimberley found themselves jumping like mad at the best Busted show in the world.

Afterwards Sabrina got a kiss from them (on the lips). Her star wish had come true.

Maia Paul (12)
St Ives School, Cornwall

The Owl

Cara was an orphan until Jenny adopted her. One morning she remembered to ask Jenny about the owl that sat outside her window every night. Jenny told her that the owl used to be her son's but he'd died and it had been set free. Cara murmured that the owl had sounded sad. Jenny thought it was missing him.

'You poor thing,' Cara whispered as she slipped open the window.

The owl suddenly realised she was there and it gave three sharp squawks and pushed a mouse towards her.

'There, who's clever?' Cara said softly. The owl dipped its head and Cara began to tickle it.

Each night, the owl would come and Cara would fuss over it. Finally one night the owl arrived with another owl. Cara just sat and then understanding, Cara followed the owl to a barn. High in the rafters was a nest with an owl and baby chicks. Her owl was no longer alone.

Annabel Nicholas (12)
St Ives School, Cornwall

A Day In The Life Of A Victim

I'm a victim, a victim of neglect, loneliness, sadness, the brutal fists of the people I thought I knew. If you ever ask anyone for help or advice, you'll always get the same reply - you should talk to someone you trust.

But when there is no one, where do you go then? Where do you turn to when the teachers ignore you, when your parents are never there or, when they are, they're shouting, hitting and throwing things at you? Who do you turn to when you can't trust anyone, when your so-called friends hit and kick you or let others, and tell you the truth about the horror that is you?

I learned how to survive the hard way. If you look hard enough in the class of kids, you might spot me, it's safer not being noticed. I'm the plain one, the one with bags under my eyes, bruises on my face and neck. These days I'm as pale as snow, shaking, jumpy. They made me this way and they'll carry on, no one will stop them.

As they beat me, I realise something's different, it doesn't hurt, it can't - inside I'm already dead.

This was my life, it ends tonight. I hope that with this, my life won't have been completely worthless, that others like me get proper help, not just the theory. I've decided to go in my sleep. I will never see morning. My hands don't shake as I pick up the pills.

I'm peaceful at last.

Hanna Benney (14)
St Ives School, Cornwall

The Loch Ness Monster

'Can we go camping in the holidays, Mum?' Tally said, brushing her sister, Carly's hair.

'Yeah,' shouted Carly.

'That's a good idea,' their mother answered.

'But where?'

'Loch Ness,' Carly said.

'Loch Ness it is then,' Mum answered.

That weekend they packed up their stuff and started off on their journey to Scotland. After two hours, they arrived at the campsite. Mum put up the tent while Tally and Carly ran down to the loch with their brand new fishing rods.

Suddenly Tally jumped. 'I just saw a massive fin come out of the water, look.'

'Oh shut up Tally, sit down, don't be stupid,' Carly paused, 'oh my God, I said I wanted to find the Loch Ness monster but I didn't mean it.'

'Quick Carly, grab the camera, take a picture,' shouted Tally.

Click.

'Got it,' said Carly.

'Look, she's jumping up into the air!' Tally said, amazed.

'Wow, let's watch her for a bit,' said Carly.

After two hours, Tally realised what time it was. 'Come on, we'd better get back,' she said.

'And become famous, we have a photo of the Loch Ness monster,' Carly added happily.

Tally answered, 'I don't think we should give anybody the picture.'

'What?' said Carly, shocked.

'There'll be loads of people swarming around here. She'll never get any peace.'

'I agree,' Carly agreed and she threw the photo into the loch and the monster jumped out of the water.

'Bye Lotty,' the twins said as they walked away.

Zoe Everson (13)
St Ives School, Cornwall

Rebecca's Fight For Survival

I stood solemnly staring at the train and fiddling with the name tag around my neck. I felt fearful and refused to let go of my brother's hand. He was crying into the misty morning air.

The train was damp and derelict, it trundled along the track, winding a path through the countryside.

'When will we get there?' moaned William. 'I'm tired and I'm cold and I'm hungry!'

'You've said that already,' I pointed out irritably.

As we arrived at our destination, many of the passengers on the train started weeping uncontrollably. I couldn't though. I had to set an example. Mum made me promise, just before she died.

Our new home for the next few weeks was to be a little town called St Ives. It was my dream to holiday there, but now wasn't the time. Also it was the middle of winter.

Finally we found ourselves with a stranger, fighting to stay sane. We had never experienced such an appalling time. Throughout the days, we would sit and watch the clouds, and at night, lie awake hoping for news from London.

When we did finally return home, it was a dreadful sight. Derelict and collapsed buildings littered the horizon. We were alone.

Dad was dead. Mum was dead, and we didn't have any family to speak of, but we had to survive. It was a matter of life and death. Literally.

Florence Weatherly (12)
St Ives School, Cornwall

The Chair

My name is Annabelle. I live in a small bungalow and have a small bedroom.

Mother and Father cannot afford for me to go to school. My brother Ross is a writer who loves Shakespeare and often plays with me. I love Ross ever so!

I have never left my home due to an illness which leaves me weak. Mother refuses to tell me what it is and rarely allows me to leave my bedroom. My right leg does not move properly and Ross has to help me about.

The dinner today was stewed cabbage. Ross served it to me and said that he was going out for a few hours. When I asked what for, he said that it was a secret. He opened my window and I felt the fresh spring air on my face. I longed to dance in the long green grass of the distant fields, and skip around the hedges and trees. When I turned to Ross, he had vanished and I heard my parents arguing in the kitchen.

I leant back in bed and shut my eyes. I dreamt I was riding a beautiful white unicorn. We were flying over valleys and mountains with the wind blowing through my hair.

Suddenly I awoke to loud crashes. Ross appeared with a big grin on his face. He pushed a chair on wheels through my bedroom door. He had made it for me. He lifted me into it and wheeled me to the wonderful world outside.

Sarah Fuller (11)
St Ives School, Cornwall

A Lost Child

Children cry for their mothers, wanting to get back home. They're lost in the middle of nowhere, fighting for their lives. Crying and screaming for their brothers and sisters to save them from all the banging, crashing, and all the explosions. It's horrible for them and they know how much they want to get back to their loving families.

Their families are poor but they are loved. They don't care about their clothes, the amount of money they have, or where they live.

The little boy is still lost, he is petrified and alone. The explosions carry on going and it's not nice. This little boy looks around, his teeth chatter with fear. It's impossible to last this long in the war. He carries on looking around through the smoke and dust. Suddenly he spots a familiar face. He runs! He is happy because he has found his mother and his life.

She is all beaten up. He asks her what's wrong. His mother lies there in his arms, trying to breathe, but it's impossible. His father runs over, hugs his son, looks at his wife and cries. It's just the father and son together. The explosions have stopped, it has all gone quiet.

The boy wonders who did this to his mother and why. They pray for themselves, each other and for themselves, each other and for the soul of their mother.

Hannah Rae (11)
St Ives School, Cornwall

The Cloud Chamber

The scintillating tower of velvet blue punctuated by glittering stars loomed high in the sky. It seemed to soak up light and emit it with regenerated brilliance. Every month, a group of strange men gathered there. Most of them arrived by just appearing out of thin air - they all wore grand, sweeping cloaks. Some said they came just to gaze at clouds, hence the name, the Cloud Chamber. However the truth is far more dangerous.

One day, Billy, a lean, dark-haired boy was wandering aimlessly around his home village: He was lonely - he just didn't belong. He looked up to the Cloud Chamber, walking towards it. Billy felt at home whenever he was there.

After the short trek, Billy walked around to the entrance. Suddenly he froze. There, standing in front of him, was a wizened old man in a long, sweeping cloak. Billy turned to run away, but the man commanded him, 'Come here!'

His legs slowly lifted up. Billy's brain screamed at his leg to stop moving, but it was oblivious to everything except the man.

Billy stood at the great iron gate, the entrance to the cloud chamber.

The old man's voice said, 'I am from a magical dimension, this is the portal to that dimension. You belong there!'

Billy was released from the spell as the gate swung open. 'I will come!' he shouted, sensing where he belonged. He was never seen again.

At the Eden Project, the Cloud Chamber still stands!

Oscar Williams (12)
St Ives School, Cornwall

Kraznier

The dungeons of Castle Krill were lonely, sad places where the corridors were full of memories and mutilated bodies where screams and moans bled from every crack and crevice of the damp, mossy walls.

The castle dungeons smelt of foul, rotting carcasses and were permanently cast in shadow. Somehow we had to escape, so we devised a plan. It took us several minutes to plan, but it was made easier by a map that Doughty had brought with us.

First I crept through an empty room. As I approached the door, I realised that there was a guard patrolling the corridor. We decided I should go ahead since I was the quietest. As I slowly crept up behind the guard I threw a pebble just behind the door. Hearing the noise, he came to inspect, but in the blink of an eye I grabbed him. I signalled to the others to follow me and so we ventured on.

We had to go through the guards' room to collect the weapons that we needed for our journey. When we reached the guards' room I slightly opened the door and peered inside. The room was a large room with wooden beds at the sides. It was cold and damp and the walls were mossy. The air smelt musty and there was an essence of beer. It was dim and the only light was a flickering candle held by the only awake guard who was glaring at me unblinkingly.

Jed Winstone (13)
St Ives School, Cornwall

Yeti

'Are we nearly there yet?' asked Tammy turning her Walkman off and looking out the car window.

'Yeah this journey's getting boring!' exclaimed Jan folding her arms.

'Oh! Stop moaning, we are nearly there just a couple of yards,' she announced combing her hair into a ponytail.

'Here we are!'

'Mum! Can we go for a walk?'

'Yes of course, but be careful!'

'Yeah! We will!' they shouted, rushing into a cave.

'What do you think we'll see?' asked Jan clutching her camera.

'Don't know, something interesting I hope!'

'Yeah! That would be great!'

'Hey! Tammy, what's that over there?'

'Don't know, want to go over and have a look?'

'Yeah of course!'

'What is it?'

'I think it's a . . . !'

'Yeti!' they both shouted at the top of their voices.

'Quick, take a picture of it!'

'Okay!'

Click.

'Got it, now let's go!'

'Great, now we have got a picture to show to people at home!' exclaimed Jan in an excited way.

'Come on, let's go now, Mum'll be wondering where we're are!'

'Jan!'

'Yeah!'

'Don't show anyone the picture!'

'OK, but why?'

'Because the poor thing will never have peace!'

'Okay'

'Good now let's go back.'

'Hello girls, did you have a nice walk?'

'Yeah! We saw a . . . !'

Tammy nudged Jan and continued, 'A bear, we saw a bear!'

'Oh! Right, got any pictures?'

'No!'

'Oh, that's a shame!'

'Yeah!' said Jan, clutching the picture.

'What was that picture in your hand just then . . . ?'

Sophie Reavill (13)
St Ives School, Cornwall

Amnesia

Have you ever had one of those days when you were in the wrong place at the wrong time? Jackson had found the violent neighbourhood while strolling through the city. He didn't know it then, but this was the end to his life as he knew it - the wrong place at the wrong time.

On the ground lay an unknown man, unable to move. His body was set in a rigour of blinding hot pain - he had been shot. Was it possible he was still alive? But his thought track returned to the man he saw before he fell; a smart lawyer type. What was he doing here? He didn't belong. He had seen Jackson run off, only to be struck down by his assassin.

The slits of Jackson's eyes opened to reveal rows of vivid fluorescent lighting, and an intense clinical smell. He was in hospital. It was a real blow to the head, and he felt it now. A nurse had filled him in - he was brutally hit on the head by thugs, and the unknown man had died, making him an eyewitness to murder. What was she talking about - how could he be? He couldn't even remember his own name.

Jackson returned to the crime scene - the place where it had all begun; only this time he had no memory or recollection of *anything.* He thought this might help, but he felt nothing. What could he do? Where did he go from here?

Nicola Goodman (15)
St Ives School, Cornwall

Sabretooth

Paul, a thirteen-year-old computer whizz-kid and criminal mastermind, had just pulled the pin of a gas grenade and thrown it through the window above the door. Paul counted to five then he put on his gas mask and walked right in like he owned the place, turning off the CCTV cameras as he went past.

The rest of the team turned on the time machine and set the time to 'prehistoric'. Paul went down to the lab but there was no one there. Paul heard a trickling, so he followed the noise, noticing that it was getting louder and louder. A shadow ran across the wall. Paul moved into the shadows and worked his way down to the small, narrow walkway. A drip landed on his head. He jerked back and stuck his hand out. A drip of blood skimmed his fingertips. He put his finger to his nose and smelt the blood - it was human!

Paul crept down the narrow hallway. He heard a noise; a growling, prowling noise. A foot came around the corner, followed by a snout and on the front of the snout were savage yellow teeth. Blood-red eyes peered around the corner. It carried on going past. It stopped and its head turned and looked at Paul. Paul was so terrified that he couldn't open his mouth or move his legs. It moved towards Paul, getting faster and faster. Paul screamed. Great big yellow teeth grabbed his head and slammed his body down with its paw. Blood sprayed all over the place. Limbs were torn and thrown around like dogs' toys.

'Paul, Paul! You're dreaming, wake up,' Mum said.

'A dream Mum?' said Paul. 'But it looked so real!'

Aron Gray (12)
St Luke's High School, Devon

My Big Day

It was the morning of a big match. I was excited to see what happened when I played for the final match of the season. I got to the ground and warmed up to play the game. Then the manager told us where we were going to play. I was going to play up front.

Then the other team turned up. After 5 minutes we kicked off. We were at home at King George V football ground. At the end of the match the score was 7-2 to us. In the added time I got passed the ball and took it past 3 defenders and I was dribbling and had a shot and I scored! All of my team came around and they were clapping me and saying well done. Then the final whistle went and we went away with the cup. The other people who scored were Jacky who scored a hat-trick and Gaby who scored two goals!

After the game, we were given the cup and it was given to our captain. We are very proud of winning the cup. After the game we all went out to celebrate at a pub and we had a very nice time.

Jade Gillard (12)
St Luke's High School, Devon

The Marriott Hotel

It was on the 19th March that I went to the Marriott Hotel. When I arrived it looked brilliant from the outside and when you went in it looked even better. There was a man to take up your bags to your room for you. He took us to our room and gave us a key card each so we could get in and out of our room.

When we opened our door we were stunned by the size of the room for 4 people, it was huge. They left us some complimentary chocolate chip cookies and a guide on how to get to the swimming pool, which was on the second floor, at the end of the corridor and then type in your secret password. Mine was ********. So if you feel like going you can type in my password, that's if you know it, *ha ha ha!*

One night, on the night I went out, I ran home from the restaurant and I went into my hotel room before the others and changed into my pyjamas, got all the quilts and duvets then ran to the elevators. I sat in one of the elevators and then it started to go down. When I got to the bottom my dad said, 'What are you doing?'

I said, 'Sleeping in the elevator,' so I did.

I woke up in the morning and the receptionist gave me *breakfast in the elevator!*

Alex Humphries (13)
St Luke's High School, Devon

The Boy

Those eyes. I'll never forget those eyes; they shot right through me like a bullet from a gun. The lightest blue, but with no sparkle in them, like dead eyes. I'll start from the beginning, so you understand.

It all began when I started high school. I was fine at first but after about three weeks the dreams started. Dreams like none I've ever had before. There were three dreams, each one scary but different, apart from one thing. This boy was in every dream - a skinny little blond kid with blue eyes. He never helped me in the scary dreams though, he just watched.

I told Laura and Emily about the dreams. They laughed at first, they thought I was joking. But they saw by the look on my face I was deadly serious. I told them about the boy. Then we started to see things, not in our imaginations but real things, things that moved for no reason.

In our school we have big, heavy oak doors in the corridor, you have to use most of your body weight to move them. We came back from lunch one day and we saw one of them move, no one had touched it, it just swung just as we got near it. There was no breeze so it couldn't have been that. Then we saw him, the boy from my dreams; a ghost. Then he disappeared from my dreams.

Laura Sacre (13)
St Luke's High School, Devon

Laura's Dance

It was a lovely hot day. The carnival was in town so I decided to go and watch it with my friends. That was the first time I saw Laura dancing as a majorette. I decided I would like to join the majorettes and become friends with Laura.

The next day I joined the majorettes and met Laura. As the weeks went on we became best friends.

Finally my dream came true and the following year I was dancing as mace in the carnival next to Laura.

Jade Lewis (12)
St Luke's High School, Devon

A Day In The Life Of David Beckham

Hello, this is the guide to the life of David Beckham and I will tell you what he does in a day.

He wakes up, has his breakfast and drives his car to Real Madrid training ground where he trains until about 12 o'clock, lunchtime. Then he goes home to his beautiful wife Victoria and the kids, Brooklyn and Romeo.

He goes shopping for designer clothes and buys a Calvin Klein outfit and Victoria buys a posh dress. When he's finished shopping, he has a kick about with the kids and then they go home to get changed before they all go out for a meal.

They go to a very posh restaurant for a meal and David and Victoria eat spaghetti Bolognese, while the children eat fish and chips.

They leave the restaurant at 6pm and when they step outside the paparazzi are waiting for a photograph of David, Victoria and the two kids. The press take photographs as David tries to cover Brooklyn and Romeo with his coat.

When they get home, they put the kids to bed so they can watch TV in peace and quiet.

It sounds great and I wish I had a life like that!

Chris Hutchings (13)
St Luke's High School, Devon

I Fell Pregnant At 13

I went out with this boy called Dan when I was 12 and on my 13th birthday I had a party. All my mates and Dan came round to my house. I was allowed one of my friends round to stay the night cos my mum had work and I didn't want to be alone on my birthday. So I asked Tasha if she wanted to stay the night. She said yeah.

We all had a bit much to drink but when the others went me and Tasha got out a year's supply of alcohol. Then there was a knock at the door. I went to answer it and it was Dan and his mate Jake, they were both drunk. I knew my mum wasn't coming back for another four hours at least so I let them in.

Dan said he had come to give me my birthday present, and he said that it was very romantic. He said, 'Come on, let's go to your room.'

So I did and that is when it all went wrong.

A few weeks later I found out but I knew I had to keep it.

8 and a half months later I had a healthy baby girl weighing just 4.6 pounds.

Samantha Marshall (12)
St Luke's High School, Devon

A Holiday To Remember

Simon was a 22-year-old tourist who had visited every country, except for Britain.

'Hi there, I am Simon.'

'Nice to meet you Simon. There will be a taxi outside of the airport any second, so enjoy your time here in Exeter,' said the airport worker.

'Thank you.'

3 hours later

'Right, that will be £4.72 please,' said the taxi driver.

Simon handed him the money. 'Thank you.'

The taxi drove off and Simon walked down the road to meet his landlord.

'Hi, I'm Simon,' Simon said whilst holding out his hand for a friendly shake.

'Hi Simon, I'm Fred your landlord, come on in my boy.'

When Simon got to the house Fred showed him around his new home. Simon unpacked and went to explore Exeter. He met up with a girl, Michelle. They talked for a few hours and then said goodbye, until tomorrow.

Simon sat down on the beach. 'I have made two new friends, nothing can spoil my day now.'

'Wrong pal!' said a gangster from behind.

The gangsters held Simon for ransom. They rang Fred the landlord, and told him that he was being held ransom for £22,000.

Fred met up with Michelle and they both got the money sorted. Fred put the money outside and the gangsters collected it. Simon was tied up outside the back.

Simon was tired of Britain already so he packed his bags, said his goodbyes and got back to the airport!

Daniel Mcloughlin (13)
St Luke's High School, Devon

City's Point Threat Lifted

Exeter City's 10-point deduction is lifted.

Today Exeter City Football Club were relieved to hear that the possible threat of a 10-point deduction has been quashed.

Both fans and officials expressed their joy at the news that their beloved club had escaped the deduction that had threatened to derail this season's push for promotion.

The points deduction scare had come into place as Exeter had gone into CVA (corporate volunteer agreement) because of their failing finances. One fan commented on the matter, 'It has been a ginormous relief to everybody in the club that this scare has gone and now we can concentrate on the league'.

Exeter are currently lying in 6th in the Nationwide Conference and with some of the major rivals slipping up at the weekend, the future looks, if a little cloudy, very much brighter.

There is still a threat that they will be deducted 36 points for the transfer of Dwane Lee after the transfer embargo.

Matthew Webb (13)
St Luke's High School, Devon

No Appeal For Soccer Star: Rio Says No More Appealing

Manchester United star centre back, Rio Ferdinand, has said no more appealing for his drugs test the star missed. The England star told us that he's had enough of all the nonsense, he just wants to let it go and fly right over his head.

Rio will fail to take part in the remainder of Manchester United's failing season. Not only will the centre back miss the rest of the season, he will miss England's Euro 2004 campaign in Portugal.

He will return from his 8 month ban on 20th September 2004 which will rule him out of the start of the 2004-2005 season. After we interviewed the gutted centre back, Rio Ferdinand, we interviewed his former Manchester United colleague David Beckham and he said, 'We're all very disappointed that Rio can't play in Euro 2004 but we'll just have to get on with it'. Although David said he and his teammates were very disappointed, he said, 'We need players of nearly his ability to play alongside Arsenal's powerhouse defender Sol Campbell, like Chelsea captain John Terry or the very experienced Middlesbrough centre back Gareth Southgate'.

There is always the less experienced defenders like Ledley King and Anthony Gardner from Spurs or Jonathon Woodgate and Titus Bramble. But the main question is will Sven pick the right men?

Billy Rouse (12)
St Luke's High School, Devon

The Story Of The Skateboarder

Hi, I am Tony Hawks. I started skating when I was very young. Now I am going to fight for the championship of the world tomorrow. I am flying to Florida to become champion of the world.

Now I am waiting at the airport for my flight.

It is now time to get on my flight. I will see you later in Florida.

Now I am at Florida, I am so excited. From the airport it is half an hour drive to the skate park and I am sure I am going to win the world championship. See you at the park.

I am outside the park now, waiting to go in. I am so excited, I can't explain. See you inside.

I am in the park now, just about to skate and I am positive I am going to win.

'Tony Hawks, please come to the ramp of death.'
His trick is a barrel roll.
'Please step up and do your trick.'

'Here are the results.'
Tony Hawks wins.
'Oh and look at this, he is dancing with joy. Come on Tony, come and collect your prize.'

Tony rings up his mum and says, 'I've won.'
She faints with joy.

Byron North (12)
St Luke's High School, Devon

A Day In The Life Of . . .

'A day in the life of . . . ' is a topic that gets most people thinking. Those six words can spark off ideas in the dullest person's mind. On hearing that phrase, even the most unimaginative person will be thinking, *who can I write this about?* And away they go. But then there are the people who don't. Who, after thinking long and hard about who is interesting enough to write a story about, still draw a blank. It is these people that I can sympathise with. It is these people that I can look at and say, 'God, it's irritating isn't it?'

See, people who do get suffocated by inspiration at the mere mention of that phrase will never be able to understand the sheer torture of having a perfectly good topic and finding out that their muse has packed up and gone to Jamaica. It just isn't fair when everyone else is writing about 'A day in the life of . . . Squirrel the squirrel', or 'Monkey the monkey', or even something more ambitious like 'Frank the frankfurter sausage', and the only thing you can come up with is your name and the title, neither of which was thought up by you.

And so now to the point of my incessant rambling, I have to say something: You are not alone! I too am plagued by the vast nothingness that fills my head and yet I can ramble on for 250 words. Who'd have thought it?

Annie Langley (14)
St Luke's High School, Devon

A Day In The Life Of A 14-Year-Old

Well, it is pretty boring really but some days I might be lucky and something exciting might happen. When it does there's no stopping it. The last time something exciting happened was about five months ago, on the 20th December to be exact. It had been snowing for a whole week non-stop. I don't really like the wet, cold, hard, horrible snow so I try to stay inside.

Three weeks later, when it still hadn't stopped, the streets were blocked with snow up to my knees.

'Help! Help!' said a faint, muffled voice.

It was coming from the snow. A rush of danger came over me. I tried to run and find the voice in the snow. I tried shouting, but the voice still sounded far away.

I kept running and running till the voice sounded closer, and there by my feet was a small girl who was cold and blue.

'Hello. Hello. Can you hear me? What is your name?'

But the girl just lay there. Panic struck me but I still stayed calm and rang 999.

About 15 minutes later I was carrying the still-blue girl through the snow to the clear road where an ambulance was waiting.

'Are you OK?' asked the paramedic as he looked at me.

'Umm, umm, fine, fine.'

I slowly walked back to my house and warmed up.

An hour later the phone rang; the blue girl was fine.

What an experience.

Luann Bennellick (14)
St Luke's High School, Devon

My Life As A Panda

My life is fun and boring. I wake up every morning and search around for food, mostly bamboo shoots or sticks. I eat mostly all day and I sometimes like to crouch up in a ball. I like to climb trees. Most of the time I like to play fight, sometimes with my brother, sisters and friends. I like eating bamboo. It's my favourite, that's why I like eating it so much.

I can climb trees and sometimes I see wonderful views. I can rest up in a tree, and I like watching the sun set before I go to bed.

In the morning I climb down from my tree. I don't really have a home, I roam around and if I like the spot I'm in, I stay there.

Then I sit down and eat loads of bamboo sticks - they're healthy for me, it's part of my diet. I find new friends to play with then I go back to find more food before I go to bed.

I rest up high in a tree where no other animals can get to me. I rest nice and peacefully up in my tree.

Adam Williams (13)
St Luke's High School, Devon

A Day In The Life Of James Coppinger (Exeter City Player)

The fans, the manager, the players are all great at Exeter.

I am settled here and don't want to move to another club. I am playing the best football of my life. The fans cheer me on with my own songs and many people haven't got their own chant, but me, Sean Devine and Steve Flack do.

I am best mates with all the players at Exeter. They are great players and my mates. It would be better if we were allowed to have a drink for a night but the manager is strict on that.

Gareth Sheldon has done great to come back to match fitness.

Today I have a match against Leigh RMI. It's ten o'clock and I am just having my breakfast and psyching myself up for the match, that's what I also do. It's time to go to the stadium now for pre-match preparations with the manager and players.

The away team just arrived to play and I'm trying to psych them out

It's about ten minutes to kick-off now and I'm drinking my Lucozade which makes me last 33% longer out on the pitch.

We are walking out now and the fans are singing. It looks like three to four thousand are here today, but the atmosphere is better than Man United's.

We kick-off first and we are shooting towards the away end.

It's 1-0 to Leigh RMI in the first half, but we are ready to fight back to keep us on trail to play-offs.

At full-time we've won 3-2, we scored two late goals.

After the match we go for a warm down out on the pitch.

I'm on my way home now to get my tea and go to bed.

Martin Davis (14)
St Luke's High School, Devon

My Life As A . . .

This is my life as a dolphin.

Hi, my name is Flipper, Flipper the dolphin. I have loads of brothers and sisters. We all swim around all day. Most people that see us say that we have skin that is like a sponge - a soft, wet sponge.

We have loads of people surrounding us, giving us little fish to eat.

The ranger always comes in a boat and talks to the visitors and tells them what our habitat is.

The most fun thing is when people pay more money to come and swim with us. We get the feel of different people's smooth or rough hands on our smooth fins.

The water is a clear crystal-blue when the sun is shining down on it.

Our trainers/rangers tell us to jump over a wire or go up to little children and then with their little hands and fingers they touch our spongy skin. We get people all ages coming to see us. We are so intelligent, that is why people from all countries love to see us swim and do tricks.

I love being a dolphin!

Emma Belcher (14)
St Luke's High School, Devon

My Life As A Gorilla

This is the life of a gorilla.

My life as a gorilla is a very wild experience. Every day I get woken by the leader, the silverback. Making sure that we don't have any company with any poachers or strange researchers, we then eat.

All day me and my family sit around eating and grooming. As the rain falls down we all begin making a nest using leaves and leftovers.

Some days people from all over the world come to research and analyse our lives, but it's not always like that, we get chased by poachers with horrid and scary thoughts.

That's how my family gets smaller and smaller. Our population is going down, by this, for money.

It's time for bed, the whole family is silently asleep.

Michelle Wills (14)
St Luke's High School, Devon

Zack And The Pizza

A bloke in his mid-twenties called Zack, was riding home on his moped from Valor, where he worked one pleasant April evening when his phone rang. He pulled over to the side of the road, took his mobile out of his right trouser pocket and answered it. 'Hello?' he said as if it were a question.

'Hi mate,' replied the voice, 'it's Will.'

'Oh, hi Will,' said Zack.

'I was wondering if you would like to go climbing at the university later,' asked Will, 'I've just called Zeek and he's going to meet us there.'

'Sounds like a great idea,' responded Zack, 'and maybe we could go for a pizza afterwards,' he suggested.

'Yeah, cool,' Will agreed, 'so, I'll meet you at the uni at about 8.30?'

'Yeah, OK,' said Zack. 'See you later.' And he hung up.

Zack went home, got changed, collected his climbing gear and got into his car. He was really excited because he'd got a new harness and wanted to try it out. He started the engine and headed for the uni.

When he got there, Will and Zeek were waiting for him at the bottom of the wall.

'Come on then,' said Will, 'let's go.'

They had a great climb and afterwards went to Pizza Hut and shared a big Hawaiian pizza with 'cheese-filled crust' and enjoyed it very much indeed.

When Zack got home he thought, *what a fantastic evening.* He sighed, sat down and poured himself a double whisky.

Simon Johns (12)
St Luke's High School, Devon

A Day In The Life Of A Cat

After prowling the streets at night I could smell the food coming through the cat flap up to my nose. It was like a rope dragging me into the house.

As I got closer the smell of the beef and the gravy was getting stronger. As I stepped through the cat flap there it was, the beef and gravy waiting for me like a chest of treasure.

After I'd eaten my food I could feel the chill of the cold air coming through the cat flap and it made me want to sleep by the fire. I went to sleep and all of a sudden I heard this big bang, I jumped and my heart was pounding like something had happened to me. I could smell something strange like a piece of burnt toast. I looked behind me and I saw my tail on fire . . .

Mrrowww! All of a sudden I ran out of the cat flap and I looked for a puddle. Instead I found someone with a drink and he dropped it and put the fire out instantly. 'Miaow, what luck.'

Always remember that fires can be warm but sometimes too warm.

Jay Passmore (12)
St Luke's High School, Devon

A Day In The Life Of Hurmy-Truide

Buck hi my name is Hurmy-Truide. I am a female chicken and I am going to tell you what I do for a living.

In the mornings I wake up clucking at around 5.30am to get my slimy but tasty worms and bugs.

I have two squirrel mates and they are called Bill and Ben the squirrel pot men. My friends take the mickey sometimes because I have one leg. The other leg had arthritis, so I had to have it taken off so now I have a stump there. Anyway enough about me more on where I live and who I live with.

I live near Burnthouse Lane in Exeter, Devon and my family is just my mum, Ben my brother, Gemma my sister, Blaine my other brother, Amber my sister and Callum my third brother.

My best time of the week is either Mondays or Sundays because we go shopping on Sundays at Tesco and we go in town on Mondays. But my mum is busy at the moment because she is building me a pen, so at the moment I live in a summerhouse.

I have a best mate called Fred the spider, but he lives on the other side of the garden so I have to hobble across there but after a while I have to have a rest because it gets painful, but if I do make it across without any help or rest I will succeed in being strong like that advert on TV 'Sure she can fight but can she do her own stunts?'

Around 11.30am I am tired anyway because I am an egg layer. I lay around seven or eight weekly, so it is quite painful as it is like an elephant squeezing through a cat flap!

Amber Corcutt (14)
St Luke's High School, Devon

Scram And The Pie

Scram was an alley cat who lived in a rusty old dustbin, in the centre of a large cul-de-sac on the outskirts of Leeds.

The colour of his coat was an unusual colour. It was almost a dark blue, but it had a grey streak going through it now and then. Around his neck he wore a black collar with a silver bell which dangled down at the front of his neck. His eyes were the same colour as his coat.

On a late Monday afternoon, Scram was walking through a row of houses when he came across a large pie sitting on a window ledge. Scram hadn't had his breakfast and was very hungry from not having anything to eat the night before.

He turned his head slowly to the left and then to the right, making sure no one was coming (by this time he was dribbling all over the floor). He pounced on the pie knocking it off the window ledge and splattering it all over the freshly cut grass. He tried a bit and spat it back out. It was apple pie (his least favourite).

Mrs Phillips (the owner of the house and pie) came running out, realising what had happened.

Scram got the fright of his life, when he was hit on the back with a broomstick and pushed out of the garden.

From then on Scram decided never to try or take anything unless offered (especially home-made pie).

Jade Lynch (13)
South Molton Community College, Devon

My Younger Life Was Destroyed!

I got my first spot at 11. At first, I didn't think much of it, as I knew it was just part of getting older - hormones changing. I started to worry, as they became more noticeable. By the time I was 13 my face was covered in little bumps. I felt terrible. No one else in my school had half as many spots as me. Every time I looked in a mirror, I'd just want to curl up and die. Everyone would call me 'Pizza face'. I'd try to get even with them by putting them down on their clothes and looks. It didn't make me feel any better though.

I was so jealous of my mates when they flirted with all the boys. I had no confidence. 'Why would boys like me?' I'd say to myself. 'I'm just an ugly pizza face.' My mates would try to set me up with some boys, but no one would. It got to the stage where I couldn't approach other children. My parents got me home-tutored. It was so much easier for me as I could concentrate more on education rather than looks.

Two years later, when I started college, I was all cleared up. I got on well with everyone, in fact my first week I was invited on a date. My life has totally changed.

Melissa Ackland (13)
South Molton Community College, Devon

Hairy Botty And The Order Of The Double Velvet

After Rolldemort returned, Hairy Botty returned to Drunken Potty Way where he lived along with his Aunt Germia, Uncle Curdle and his cousin Bogey. Hairy Botty was considered a liar in the world of bitches and lizards, because everybody didn't want to believe that Rolldemort had returned.

When Rolldemort was at the height of his powers he wreaked havoc on all of the lizarding world and even the gurgle (non-magic folk) world. He killed and killed endlessly.

Bog Rolldemort used the killing curse 'Fartacus Sewagius' which would earn you a lifetime in Asjerbanny (the lizard prison) where the Diarrhoea Eaters were.

Hairy Botty was walking down Drunken Potty Way, Rolldemort attacked Hairy Botty. Hairy Botty reflected Rolldemort's curse with the spell 'Fartacus Repellus' and Rolldemort ran away with his tail between his legs.

Then all of a sudden Honks appeared (a bitch), Mingsley appeared (a lizard), Mad-Eye Grumps and Bumblebee appeared (both are lizards), Hairy was astounded. This was the Order of the Double Velvet.

Rolldemort appeared out of the blue with all of his followers. Rolldemort shot a curse at Honks, who fell with a gasp. Quacknair, one of Rolldemort's followers, attacked Mingsley and then there was three: Bumblebee, Hairy and Grumps. Bumblebee hit Rolldemort with a body bind curse, Grumps hit Quacknair and Hairy hit Boil, another follower of Rolldemort.

There was a giant funeral for Mingsley and Honks, whereas Rolldemort, he just disappeared. Will Rolldemort wreak havoc once again on the lizarding world?

Mark Brooks (12)
South Molton Community College, Devon

A Day In The Life Of Frankie Dettori

'Hurry up, the race is gong to start in five minutes!' I pulled my blue silks over my head and fastened my collar with a safety pin, the cuffs were already rolled and fastened with an elastic band. My breeches were hung on a peg alongside my boots; I slipped them on and tucked myself in to look neat.

On the way out I grabbed my hat and ran to the ring where my ride was stood waiting for me. It was a nice-looking bay colt with a muscular chest and long powerful quarters. His name was Dubai Destination and he was an 11-4 favourite.

His owners from Godolphin helped me mount and led me down to the field, as they let me go, one shouted, 'Do your magic, Frankie!'

I slowly cantered down to the starting gates.

It was a hot day and the sun was beaming on my back, making me sweat.

Down at the starting gates I chatted to a jockey who was also riding a favourite to win, it was a grey filly called Hawk Wing.

We were called to enter the starting gates, the horses loaded perfectly.

Suddenly the gates opened and the horses bounded onto the field.

We were going at a steady gallop.

I was fifth place but going strong along the rail

We had two furlongs to travel and I was still in fifth place. All of a sudden I saw a place in front of me, I pulled out and kicked him on. Suddenly I was in front alongside Hawk Wing, we battled on all the way to the finish.

The crowd was ecstatic as I crossed the finish, and from that moment I knew I had won!

Alex Hutter (12)
South Molton Community College, Devon

Pandora's Bully

Pandora is an ordinary 11-year-old girl who loves it at school. She gets on well with the teachers and has lots of friends. She lives in the countryside with her mum and sister. Her dad is living in London and soon Pandora, with her mum and sister will be moving to live with him. Pandora is a bit worried about the move, but she wants to see her dad.

'Bye Sarah, I'll ring you as soon as I get to my dad's house.' Sarah is Pandora's best friend and Pandora will really miss her.

'Wake up Pandora, you're late for school. It's your first day, remember.'

Five minutes later Pandora runs out of her front door, with her mum. Pandora looks a right mess: she has her shirt untucked, her tie isn't tied and her hair is a state. They jump in the car and drive to school.

Pandora runs into the class to see 30 glaring faces. She sees a snigger on one of the girls' faces. Then the whole class starts laughing.

Pandora feels a tear in her eye. She feels it dripping down her cheek. As she looks around the class she sees one of the girls stand up. Pandora rubs her eyes and tries to hide her tears.

'Cry baby, cry baby,' the girl starts shouting. 'Cry baby, cry baby.'

Then one by one the class start joining in. 'Cry baby, cry baby.'

Pandora runs out of the class. She falls on the floor and bursts into tears. She can still hear the chanting going around in her head. She feels distress, dismay and fright.

Molly Petts (13)
South Molton Community College, Devon

A Day In The Life Of Hillary Duff

'OK Hillary, you're on in ten seconds!'

God, can't I have a break? These thoughts and others were going through her mind as she got into position for her showing of Lizzie McGuire.

'Man, I've been up since five o'clock filming!' Hillary felt restless and by the end of the morning she was ready for a break!

'Where shall we go for lunch?' she asked her friend as they walked around a few blocks.

'Er, there's a restaurant around the block, what do you think?'

'Yeah sure, any place will be fine as long as I can eat!' Hillary replied.

'Yes Miss, what can I get you?' came the waiter's friendly voice.

'Er, I'll have a hamburger and Coke,' replied Hillary.

'Yeah and I'll have the same, please,' was Hillary's friend's request.

'OK, that's two hamburgers and Cokes, anything else?'

'No, that's fine thanks,' came Hillary's reply.

They spent an hour having a chat and eating lunch, then headed home.

'Right Hilli, I'll see you tomorrow then!'

'Yeah, bye!' replied Hillary, then they parted waving to each other. When Hillary got home she went to her room and fell onto her bed, letting out a yawn.

'Hi Hillary, what's up? You look exhausted,' said her mother.

'Yeah, work's fun but so hard!'

'I know the feeling love,' laughed her mum. 'Are you coming down for tea?'

'No, I need a sleep, thanks though, I'll have tea later OK?' said Hillary.

'Yeah sure, that's fine love, see you later!' Her mum closed the door quietly. In no less than five minutes Hillary was fast asleep, tired out from her day!

Mary Wheelan (13)
South Molton Community College, Devon

The Minotaur

(A retelling of the original story)

The Minotaur roared, throwing back its bull's head. The king's son watched in horror and amazement as the beast thundered towards him. He drew out his sword. He knew what he must do but he could not bring himself to do it. He raised the sword. He felt the fear of the beast and shivered. He drew a deep breath. The sword tumbled to the ground, landing at his feet. The Minotaur's horns had knocked it.

He stared into the beast's grey eyes and quivered. He picked up his steel weapon. It wasn't in his nature to kill and this was cold, brutal murder. Even if it was a beast. He lowered the weapon. It glinted in the pale ghostly light from the moon.

The beast blinked. With a quick plunge the king's son stabbed the beast. Warm blood flowed over his hand. He winced. He backed away from the beast as if it would kill him.

He ran out of the centre of the maze, turning unnecessarily, and trying to find the exit. It took a couple of minutes before he admitted to himself that he was lost. The blood on his hand had congealed. He winced again. His head was throbbing and the pain and worry was taking over. He faded into sleep and dropped onto the floor. He tried to call for help but he was too feeble. He passed out into a mixture of sleep and pain.

Rebecca Kingdom (13)
South Molton Community College, Devon

Motocross Madness

It was Saturday morning, I was out of bed at 5am ready to start the day. I double-checked my motorbike and riding gear, then off we went to the race.

We arrived at Anstey a bit late so I didn't have time to get ready. My race was about to start so I started my bike and drove into the starting grid.

3, 2, 1 and I was off!

I got a great start. I was in the lead, as I turned the corner I saw a huge jump. I thought that this was a race not a freestyle race. I didn't know how to jump yet. As soon as the two wheels left the ground I knew I was in trouble.

Crash! 'Aarrgghh,' I screamed in agony. I landed on my neck and I couldn't feel my body! Mum and Dad were running towards me but when they got to me I passed out.

Next thing I know I woke up in a hospital, Mum and Dad were saying something and crying at the same time, I didn't know what they were saying. I was wearing a huge neck brace and wires and tubes were on my body! I couldn't feel my body. This worried me a lot. I started screaming and shouting because I was paralysed! A doctor came over to me and said to me if I lay still my nerves may heal! Thank God.

Christopher Warne (14)
South Molton Community College, Devon

A Day In The Life Of Gabriel Batashuta

The ordinary day for a soldier in the war is preparing to fight, and fighting. However, sometimes things happen which you don't expect. That is exactly what happened to Gabriel Batashuta, who was fighting in the Falklands War.

He had been training to fight for a while and had only started fighting in battles two weeks before. In those 2 weeks he had been involved in some small battles but one day his services were called upon to fight a bigger and more dangerous battle.

The mission was to parachute out of a plane and land in a town in the countryside. The town was small, in fact tiny, only 80-odd houses there.

The soldier was looking forward to fighting but when it came to it, it wasn't such a fun time.

It was early in the morning when the plane took 30,000 feet. Gabriel was scared on the journey. When it was time to jump he was brave. When he jumped he had the time of his life, until he got violently caught up in his parachute; it was choking him. He was so frightened, but he got a knife out and cut himself free; he started falling faster - he tried to use his emergency parachute but it wouldn't work. He had gone numb. *Thud!* That was the end of his day.

Lloyd Slee (12)
South Molton Community College, Devon

A Day's Rally Driving To Remember

Red, orange, green and I was off to a flying start and I had 2.34.123 to beat. I was almost halfway round the rally of Kenya at stage four, we were driving almost along the side of a mountain and I thought the car was accelerating more than I had my foot down. We had a 62* right hand turn coming up and when I came to decelerating the car just carried on. I said to my co-driver, 'I can't stop!'

He just replied, 'You have to, it's a two hundred foot drop down there.'

Then the track rod ends snapped because of the speed I was turning, there was no hope for us, the accelerator was still stuck and the gearbox was jammed in fourth gear at 150mph.

How could I turn? The adrenaline was pumping so fast I almost blew up. Then it happened: we went through the wall and the car started rolling over and over, I looked at the co-driver and said, 'This is it.' The car flipped and rolled over and over again. I thought it was never going to stop then I blanked out.

When we stopped I woke up but I couldn't move. My co-driver only walked out with a couple of cuts and bruises; that was because I took a massive blow to my side of the car from a tree.

Three years later and I was determined to get back out there on the rally track and drive again; all the specialists said I would never drive again but I was going to and I was going to have the same car and co-driver.

And I did and from then onwards I have been a great success in rallying and I haven't lost a rally since I started driving again.

My one ambition is to rally in Kenya again on the same rally course. By the way my name is Sam and my co-driver's name is Henry.

Tim Milton (13)
South Molton Community College, Devon

How The Horse Got The Frog In His Hoof!

Down a peaceful lane, on a quiet farm, in a wooden stable lay a beautiful horse. He was brown all over with a distinctive white star on his forehead and a black mane and tail. The majestic animal stood up, kicked the door, broke the bolt and let himself out.

The sudden noise awoke his four best friends; Fred, Felicity, Fiona and Bob (who were frogs!)

'Where are you going Henry?' said Fiona looking up to her gigantic friend.

'I'm going for a long gallop on the moor because it's a nice day!' said Henry.

'Okay!' the frogs chorused back.

As soon as Henry had left, the frogs woke up and got ready.

'Right!' said Fiona . . . 'Places please everyone!'

All four frogs zoomed around Henry's water bucket and performed a graceful, symmetrical dance. They kept on stopping and starting until they got their dance perfect.

Soon they heard Henry's clippety-clop up the lane, so they all stopped suddenly.

'Hello Henry!' said Bob.

'We've got something to show you!' said Felicity.

Henry was surprised . . . 'What is it?' he asked.

'Watch,' said Bob.

'OK.'

Henry made himself comfy in a large, soft bale of hay. The frogs spent about quarter of an hour dancing, leaping, swimming, jumping, gliding and diving, performing the same dance.

After a while they finally came to a halt.

'Well done!' said Henry.

'Thank you,' said Fiona, 'we enjoy doing it but it *really* hurts our backs!'

'We should have a back massage!' said Bob.

'My hooves really hurt from galloping!' said Henry.

'I know!' said Felicity.

They formed a huddle and took action. The frogs leapt into Henry's hooves and cushioned his hooves and when Henry walked, all four frogs got a back massage, so that is how the horse got the frog in his hoof.

Hannah Lloyd (12)
South Molton Community College, Devon

A Day In The Life Of Rio Ferdinand

I got up at seven o'clock. I was so relieved because today I found out the court has cleared me of all charges.

I got to the court at one o'clock, my court hearing started at one thirty. There were so many photographers outside waiting for me to arrive. I nearly got blinded by flashing.

It was time to go into court. I was so nervous I felt like I had butterflies in my stomach.

It was now the halfway break. I thought I had done fairly well but I didn't think I would get cleared by the FA because they were very strict. They wouldn't even let you get away from missing a training session without a fine.

They kept on asking me the same question which I had answered. The reason I missed the drugs test was that I never got a reminder saying when it was supposed to be.

The final verdict was about two minutes away. I couldn't bear the tension. I wanted them to come out and tell me the verdict. I saw them coming to tell me and it didn't look very promising. They just told me that I'm guilty and I still have to do the eight month ban which finishes in September.

I just got home; I am distraught, I can't think of eight months without playing football, at least I can still train with the team.

Daniel Strong (13)
South Molton Community College, Devon

A Day In The Life Of A Teddy Bear

Many think I'm still at night, sat gazing out the window until morning when I'm picked up and played with. However from dark fall until the glaring sun, at its lowest point, appears on the horizon, is when I come alive.

I sit on my ledge by the window, next to the curtain, as the early dawn light slowly seeps through the window. I am in the same position as the night before, as though I have never moved.

I sit there patiently waiting for the moment when she (the girl whose bedroom I share) awakens and disappears for the day.

I'm not the favourite of her teddies - that is Mr Beanie. He sleeps by her pillow on her bed. There are 10 of us in all. However I have the freedom from where I am and I'm known as the 'King of the Ledge'.

I sleep through the day whilst no one is around so they don't see my eyes shut or hear my quiet snore. When the girl and her brother arrive back at 4 o'clock I am silent and still but I see everything, every angry argument and every little lie.

Finally the night draws near and when all are in their beds that's when the other bears and I come to life.

Claire Thomas (12)
South Molton Community College, Devon

The Search Goes On For Missing Emily

Questions are still unanswered surrounding the disappearance of South Molton teenager Emily McKeen.

The 14-year-old, who was well known in the town that she was brought up in, was last seen three weeks ago in the late hours of March 13th.

Emily's disappearance became a murder investigation after her mobile phone was found in South Street earlier this week. She left a party at a friend's house in South Street at about 11.30 with a group of friends.

She was last seen when she left her friends and walked down Mill Street to go home on her own between 11.30 and 12.00. Police still need witnesses who may have seen Emily, after she had left her friends, to come forward.

House to house searches and area searches were still being carried out this week in South Molton. DCI Meadows said: 'Nothing significant has come up but we have had a very positive response from house to house calls, however we still need more information'.

Police are still piecing together important information about Emily's last movements. A couple of witnesses said that between 11.00 and 12.30 there was an argument in Poltimore Road, where Emily lives which she could have been involved in. We also know that about 11.00 someone left the party to get more alcohol.

Girl who enjoyed having fun.

Emily is well known in South Molton by sight if not by person. Described as happy and always smiling, those who know her said she is confident and mature.

Friends that knew Emily said she was always happy, she was intelligent, confident and loud. Emily was very popular and witty.

Anyone with information about Emily's disappearance can call the police incident room on: 01392 452141. Anonymous calls can also be made to Crime Stoppers on: 0800 555111.

Becca Russell (13)
South Molton Community College, Devon

Where's Steve?

One night John went to Steve's house for a sleepover. At midnight John woke up and noticed Steve's bed was empty. John got up and started to look for his mate.

He looked out of the window but all he saw was red footprints along the garden path. He heard thumping noises from down the street.

'Is that you Steve?' shouted John. But there was no answer.

He walked down the street hoping he could find Steve, but all he saw was more and more footprints leading into the forest. He heard a rustle in the bushes, he looked behind it but only more footprints. So he followed them. He saw his friend's body, it was half dead. Without knowing it, something came up behind him and attacked . . .

Allan Leary (11)
South Molton Community College, Devon

Fairy Dust

Far, far away in fairyland, lived some pale-coloured fairies. They loved it there, waking up smelling the fresh flowers, hearing the birds sing their song.

The ugly troll-like pixies with warts on their noses, wanted the fairies' land. The pixies wanted the fairies to disappear, they wanted the land so they could make it a dark and gloomy place to live in. The terrifying pixies moved into the fairies' homes and made it dark and gloomy.

The fairies pretended to move. The queen of fairies set a spell. When the dark and gloomy pixies moved in the fairies spell started to work.

The fairies' dust drifted around every corner of the land, which belonged to the fairies. The longer the pixies stayed there, the more the flowers and butterflies appeared. This made the pixies really ill, because of the bright colours. But what the pixies didn't know was the colourful fairies slept in the deep dark forest for the night.

The pixies woke up and realised their homes had been taken over by the fairies' magical and mysterious spell. The ugly pixies moved out, so the fairies could move back in that very same day. They all went back to their normal duties and remembered all the fun they'd had.

Megan Ball (12)
South Molton Community College, Devon

Stranded

'Hello!' shouted Joe.

'Hi!' yelled Toby.

'Do you want to go skateboarding with me?' asked Joe.

'OK,' said Toby.

'Then get your gear and I'll meet you in the middle of town.'

'Alright!' I'll meet you there.'

As Joe was waiting in town, Toby was having trouble finding his skateboard.

'Where is it?' complained Toby. 'Aah there it is.' Toby's late.

'Where were you?' said Joe.

'I couldn't find my skateboard,' replied Toby.

'Well come on let's go.'

Toby and Joe were on their way to the skatepark when Joe forgot where he was going.

'Are you sure you know where you're going?' whined Toby.

'Of course I know where I'm going it's just round the corner here.'

'Oh great we're lost and it's dark too,' shivered Toby.

'Stop being a baby, we will find someone who can help us,' said Joe.

'Look,' shouted Toby, 'we can get help from the person in that car.'

So they ran over to the car but little did Joe and Toby know that that car was the car that had been kidnapping kids, they're gone now!

'Excuse me,' said Toby, 'can you help us?'

'Of course I can help,' said the kidnapper, 'come in.'

Joe and Toby went in the Mercedes.

'Argh no, don't, argh,' was all you could hear. They were murdered and their bodies were dumped.

The police soon caught the kidnappers and never found the bodies, on their grave stones was, *never trust anyone!*

Chris Fook (11)
South Molton Community College, Devon

The Haunted House

It was an awful night. Thunder rumbled and lightning lit up the stormy sky, the rain lashed. The outline of a crumbling house, stood on the moonlit skyline. Inside the crumbling house was a green, wrinkled, warty witch, with her two black sooty cats. She heard laughing, chuckling really. So she peered out of her broken window, and she saw four children, two boys and two girls. They were throwing stones at her house.

'Witches stink, I hate them,' sniggered one of the defiant boys, called Will.

'I know they just turn people into frogs, ribbit, I'm a little frog, ribbit,' replied the other boy called Jamie.

The witch was having none of this. So she slivered down into the dungeon underneath the house. Then the two girls, Becky and Laura, were slowly creeping up to the house, the door opened. All the children crept in. The door slammed shut. Bats screeched. The children were startled.

It was dark, there were strange noises. A picture fell from the wall, the girls screamed. All of a sudden the floor was covered in frogs, jumping in all directions, and the noise 'ribbit, ribbit' was deafening. Terrified, the children fled from the house, frightened they would be turned into frogs. All they could hear was the cackle of the witch, as they ran as fast as they could.

Ellie Marley (11)
South Molton Community College, Devon

Goodbye Ellie!

'Argh!' she screamed as she fell in the lake, I watched as she sank to the bottom as her blonde hair sprayed in the crystal clear water. Did I just do that? Did I just push my own best friend off the edge of the lake? I started to cry as I got on my bike to go home. It only happened because she called me 'chicken' and 'wimp'.

At 7.00 that day I watched the news, when they said the headlines I heard them mention about Ellie. They said, 'Now on to some tragic news. A young girl has gone missing. Her name is Ellie Roberts.' My face dropped. I burst into tears and ran upstairs. I just sat there crying. I then went to bed but I couldn't sleep. I kept seeing images of Ellie saying, 'Thanks a lot Louise, some friend you are, thanks a lot.'

The next day after school I told my mum and dad I was being bullied at school. Mum suggested I went and lived with my gran and grandad, so I did. But when it came to night I still kept seeing images of Ellie. So I went downstairs in the kitchen, got my grandad's gun, went to the river where Ellie died. *Bang!*

Danielle McLean (12)
South Molton Community College, Devon

The Adventure By The Sea

The sharp ear-breaking whistle of the train pulling into the station excited the four adventurous girls. The blue-painted train's doors flew open. The passengers crowded into the carriages and the train set off. The four girls sat around a table.

'I can't wait,' said Pippa excitedly.

'I hope the view is nice from the farmhouse,' said Emma.

'We might stay in a shed,' joked Jess, the others laughed.

An hour or two later they arrived at the secluded farm and met the farmer's wife.

'Hello there lovies, your bedroom is up the stairs on the right,' said the kind-hearted lady.

Next morning they investigated the caves on the beach and they found a newspaper saying: 'Smugglers strike again. Smugglers wreck another ship and take the valuable belongings. Police can't work out the mystery'.

As the girls looked further into the cave they heard footsteps ahead of them. Quietly they followed them and listened to what they were saying.

'That must have been one of the best shipwrecks ever.'

'It's a smuggler,' whispered Pippa, scared. The smugglers led them into a secret tunnel as they watched they saw it was the three main actors from the Moving Theatre that they had gone to see the night before.

Later that day Lucy and Emma told the police and made a plan to catch the people, whilst Jess and Pippa told the farmer and his wife. The police trapped and arrested the smugglers then gave back the belongings. Soon girls made their long journey home.

Sophie Lock (12)
South Molton Community College, Devon

No Longer The Centrepiece!

Inspector L Griffin, one of England's finest detectives, whether it's a murder investigation or a simple break-in, Griffin is always on the case.

One of her most favourite partners is PC Warren, always willing but not always completely right.

It just so happened that one misty morning, Griffin had just received a telephone call from Miss R Pincome, the young owner of the silversmith's, the shop assistant had been attacked and the ornate William IV centrepiece valued at £43,214 had been stolen!

'I see,' muttered Griffin, 'perhaps I should call for my superior police partner Warren?'

Griffin strolled around the shop looking for anything that could be vital evidence. Warren arrived as soon as possible, wearing his new white silk gloves. They soon started dusting for prints.

'Ah ha! Just what we're looking for.' Griffin rushed out of the shop as fast as lightning.

Later that evening;

'Dr Wilkinson, have you examined that glass yet?'

'I'm afraid so, and it leads to two suspects . . .'

Straight away Griffin headed down to the station, to see whom the forensic scientist had identified.

'Breaker Williamson, and Jewellery Thief Lock . . . I might have known.'

After many hours of questioning Griffin came to a solution:

'You see, Williamson and Lock were accompanied by the assistant who shut down the alarm before closing up. Williamson then broke in through the store window allowing Lock to steel the valuable centrepiece. They then made a quick getaway, using the assistant to cover up.'

They were all arrested.

Laura Griffin (12)
South Molton Community College, Devon

The Horror Story

It was a beautiful day. The cottage looked lovely, and close to the sea. The sun was shining and there was small waves coming in onto the beach. David and Katie were staying in the cottage with their parents. They were hoping to have a really great time.

David and Katie walked down to the beach and climbed the cliffs. Once they had got to the top of the cliffs they were really exhausted. David was teasing Katie because she was last up the cliffs and they started fighting.

An old man turned up and stopped them fighting. David and Katie got up and started chatting to the man. A great burst of wind came by and knocked Katie off the cliffs, but she was still holding on. The old man walked up to the side of the cliff and released her hands from the side, She tumbled down the side of the cliffs and lay on the beach. David was crying and worrying. Suddenly the man walked off the edge of the cliffs and lay there with Katie.

David rushed home to get his mum, his mum panicked and quickly got into the car with David and drove down to the cliffs.

David and his mum looked over the side, but no one was there. The man or Katie were not lying in the same place.

Out of the corner of his eye David saw the man and Katie happily playing in the sea.

Danny Marley (11)
South Molton Community College, Devon

Foot After Foot

Foot after foot, step after step, quickly he ran. There was no escape from the darkness. Stopping at the edge of the alley, he leant against the wall, unable to run any longer. His left arm was held across his stomach, fingers covering an ever-bleeding wound on his side. The blood dripped to the ground creating almost silent splashes in the small bloody puddle.

Tetra sat up quickly in her bed gasping for breath. She looked around the dark, poster-covered room, trying to calm down. Dreams had been haunting her since she'd moved here, some too weird to explain.

Her latest dreams weren't complete, bits of this and that, little snippets of events, none clear enough to make any sense of. They all had one thing in common though, darkness.

Tetra pulled the covers up to her chin, she didn't like the dark, now she feared it. She knew the truth. There was something out there. Waiting, feeding on those who brave the dark and enter its shadows.

A figure was walking towards a house, Tetra's house. In one swift movement they had jumped through a window. The figure landed in her room, they watched as she slept.

Tetra snapped awake once more, she looked around her room again, scared this dream could happen like the rest did. There was no one there, she sighed with relief but froze seeing a puddle of blood by the window . . . they had come for her.

Jenny Grimshire (14)
South Molton Community College, Devon

The Second Labour

In the country of Argos, long ago, was a swamp. Beside this swamp grandly stood the well of Amymone. Although it was unknown to Hercules here was to be his second labour.

For years villagers had drank the clear water from this well until one day a horrible surprise was waiting for the people, for that day the well was guarded. Beside the well, guarding it, was a monstrous creature ready to pounce on the unsuspecting passers, Hydra. Hydra was a hideous creature with nine heads, the middle of which was immortal. Try as they may no one could slay the beast so as their last hope they called Hercules.

He came, with sword in hand and in one swing cut off its head victoriously, or so he thought. But from behind came a rumble for Hydra was alive and for every head cut, two more did grow.

The beast reared up, advancing upon Hercules. Stumbling backwards, he fell to the ground searching for his sword. But the sword was nowhere to be seen. He glanced around wildly but nothing was there.

Edging backwards, something caught his eye. He turned to see a burning torch, just out of reach. He jumped up and grabbed it wildly swinging he cut right through Hydra's immortal head. He grasped it burying the head under a rock.

Victorious at last he turned with the spectators roaring, and here be the end of his second labour, but what more was to come?

Hannah-May Smith (14)
South Molton Community College, Devon

The Phoenix

This tale begins in a time of magic, of an eternal battle between good and evil. When a boy was born who would soon shake the world. His name was Tom Stone. By the age of 20 he had mastered the arts of magic and was soon renowned as leader of the forces of light against the dark. Because of this he gained the name 'The Phoenix' for this mythical bird was said to bring light in the darkness.

However, growing up it had been a thin line between good and evil which he only crossed to the good side because of the love of a lightbringer named Kate Anderton. This woman was his wife and he loved her with all his heart.

But his nemesis, known only as 'The Betrayer of Hope' leader of darkness and king of illusions, perceived this.

One day he visited Kate disguised, and persuaded her to join the darkness. When Tom heard of this he lashed out at her and destroyed her utterly, thereby condemning her to eternal torment. In doing such a thing though, he gave in to evil. Yet even as he darkened he used the remnants of his light left to cast one great spell to destroy himself, his nemesis, and to end the war by destroying both light and dark.

It is said that one day his soul shall be reborn and that of his enemy and they shall once more wage war over the same woman.

Toby Nicholas (13)
South Molton Community College, Devon

Night Of The Hunted

Ebony Riddle lay on the frostbitten earth of the cemetery, blood pouring openly from several gunshot wounds; she was deathly cold and clearly dead.

Isabella Hawke stood over her, holstering a well-used gun. She was running over her plan in her head, it would work. Of that, she was certain.

She crouched down on her hackles, blowing her corn silk hair from her eyes as she lifted Ebony from the ground, straightening up.

Stealthy as a thief, she moved from the cemetery. Nothing to show that she had been there. But blood told of her victim's, now missing, presence.

Sylvia and Hunter walked through the streets, badly written headlines from evening newspapers yelling out at them about the tragic disappearance of Ebony Riddle.

'Like, they actually care . . .' Hunter muttered sarcastically, his mind on his friend. He tossed the newspaper into the litter-choked gutter as they stalked along at an even pace.

They were tracking Ebony's scent. And, perfect, the scent led right to the well-known hangout of the discriminative hunters of the undead. Pent Forest.

Sylvia cursed foully as the forest came into sight. 'Only Hawke . . .' she hissed, her hand twitching over the hilt of her dagger as the scent of her kin's blood hit her.

The huntress, Hawke, stood in the shadows of the ancient oaks . . . her cat-like eyes watching the two. The bait, Ebony, lay next to her. Hawke was the trap. And the vampires were walking right into it. By the end of the night, her plan would be fulfilled.

To be continued . . .

Leanne Tough (13)
South Molton Community College, Devon

A Magical Surprise

Amy sat down by the water's edge and listened as a bird sang sweetly in the trees overhead. How could the world be so happy, when her day had already gone so horribly wrong? She was only given the ring yesterday and she'd already lost it somewhere!

She gazed into the crystal clear water and listened to the river's gentle bubbling. It was always so calm and tranquil here, especially in the spring; as it was now, when the ground was carpeted with bluebells and other lush spring flowers.

Suddenly, Amy sat up. Something wasn't right, but she wasn't sure what. She looked cautiously around her, wiping the tears from her cheek. She would never have imagined in her life what she was about to see, but there it was, standing just a few steps away from her, at the edge of the woodland. It was only about the size of a butterfly.

'Are you a fairy?' Amy asked, walking closer, trying to hide her disbelief.

The fairy said nothing but flew slowly over to a patch of grass nearby and stayed there, waiting. It was then that Amy saw the ring, nestling in the soft grass, the diamond gemstone sparkling wildly in the light. The fairy had found her lost ring!

Amy knelt down and picked it up, the fairy watching her every move. 'Thank you,' she whispered softly to her. 'Thank you so very much.'

Rosie Hooper (13)
South Molton Community College, Devon

The Dream

She ran through the long grass, crying frustrated tears. She blamed herself and so, it seemed, did her parents.

She reached the river bank and flung herself in the shade of a large oak tree. Memories of her and her brother Jay playing here as children entered her head, but she quickly pushed them out. Thinking of Jay was painful. She lay on her back staring up at the brilliant blue sky. The sound of the river's running water was soothing to her. The heat from the sun and the tears had made her tired. She closed her eyes and allowed herself to doze.

Over the last few weeks Lizzie's life had changed dramatically. Since the accident Lizzie could not think of a night where she hadn't dreamt of that fatal day. She was forced to relive the frightening experience every night. As she dozed, the same images haunted her dreams. She could hear the rushing water and the shouts from Jay as the treacherous water pulled him under. She saw him disappear under the surface and then reappear again, his arms flailing. She saw his terrified face as again it disappeared but this time it did not re-emerge.

She awoke suddenly in a panic. She had to help him, to save him. But it was too late. She knew he was gone.

Rachel Glover (14)
South Molton Community College, Devon

Divorce

I sat; staring at the wall in my room, praying the shouting would stop. It was so loud I was sure that the people next door would come and stop the noise, no such luck. I was so upset, I was ready to march downstairs and tell them to give it a rest. They were driving me mad, and then it stopped. Silence. Then I heard the front door slam. Dad had left.

It had been three weeks and the only way either of them would even be in each other's presence was in court talking through their lawyers. I just couldn't take it anymore, I had to get away from it all, so that night I walked out of the house, and I didn't stop walking. I must have been out all night, not knowing where I was going or where I was going to stay that night. I just hoped Mum and Dad would stop being so childish and sort it out, or was that just me being selfish?

When I came home nothing had changed. Mum and Dad still weren't talking. But there was one change, Dad was moving to America and wanted me to go with him, while Mum wanted me to stay with her.

How could they do this to me? I love them both. I can't choose.

Faye Cockram (14)
South Molton Community College, Devon

Shark Attack!

Yesterday morning, two people were attacked and killed by a great white shark off the coast of Cornwall.

The father and his young daughter went for a swim at Bude beach at 6.30am when the news spread of the missing two bodies. It is thought that the two bodies are Ben Brown and his daughter Sophie, who have not been seen since the attack.

Coastguards are searching the waters for the great beast that is thought to measure five metres long, but with no success so far.

At the moment, police are still trying to find information about these two people with the parts of the bodies that were washed to shore later on in the day, and the beaches have now been closed due to safety regulations.

PC Jones feels the situation is grave given the fact that the shark hasn't been seen since, so will it strike again tonight or tomorrow for the third kill?

Sarah Kirby (14)
South Molton Community College, Devon

It Wasn't Me

I stepped out of the car. I held my heart; I was not going to allow it to hear my fear. Its webbed feet slapped the floor making an extremely uncomfortable noise. Its grunting and sniffing sounded as if it was angry. Very angry. I asked myself, 'Does it have a weapon? Will it kill me in one blow?'

I know why it's after me; I killed its companion! I had to. Its hideous looks encouraged me to pull the trigger. But I can't seem to remember actually hitting it; I must have been too scared!

Its hands wrapped itself round the corner. I made a quick dash for it. I managed to dive behind a few pipes that smelt of something alien to me. The slapping noise had stopped. An eerie silence echoed through my swirling thoughts.

Last time I saw it, its eyes were shut. I dare not find out what's under those scaly lids.

This could not be happening. This stuff only happens in cheesy horror movies!

The sound of slapping had begun again. This time the noise was louder, almost deafening!

'This is a joke!' Maybe I am dreaming. Or maybe I am being fooled on camera. It could be one of those stupid American shows that find it humorous to scare people out of their skins!

'I can't take it anymore.' I poked my head out over the pipes. The scaly lids lifted. The beast stared straight into my eyes.

Charles Saunders (13)
South Molton Community College, Devon

A Twin Thing

It's not easy, you know? Being a fraction from a family of twelve, and being the 'one in the middle' doesn't help either. Well, joint middle actually, my twin, Josh shares the pleasure with me.

He's my best mate, Josh, we understand each other, must be a twin thing. I don't know why he went though. I feel empty. He's been gone since Monday and it's now Wednesday. You see, I just don't know why he'd run away. That's why I'm scared. Scared I've lost him forever.

Now though I've never felt more wanted in my life and I hate it. Police are asking me questions 24/7, and Mum and Dad have never talked to me so much, but whenever I say, 'He's been abducted,' they go all quiet. Then they say how stupid I was to say such a thing and that they knew he was going to run sooner or later because he'd been on his 'rebellious teen' phase for a while now. They didn't listen. They didn't feel what I felt. And they just wouldn't listen. Not until the body turned up.

Natasha McLean (14)
South Molton Community College, Devon

Village Explosion

On Saturday the 21st of August at 8.50pm, in an old barn in the small village of Rose Ash, there was a loud explosion. I know this because Mr Harvey Johnston, the nearby farmer who reported it to the police that night, told me. 'Oh it was very loud. My wife was extremely frightened, it just came out of nowhere really', he said. 'It was a shock to my wife, all the villagers and myself, nothing like that ever happens around here you know'. The loud explosion was thought to be an oil leak which then caught fire. But after the police had inspected it, it turned out to be a nuclear bomb. No one knows how it got there.

The resident of the old post office, Mrs Barbie Nicholas, witnessed a short, fat, middle-aged woman with dark brown hair, walk into the barn that same afternoon at about 2.40pm. The farmer who owns the old barn, Mr John Brook, thinks it may be his ex-wife, who got out of Dartmoor prison earlier this month, hoping to get revenge on him.

The suspect is now thought to be moving up north perhaps to the Leeds area. She is thought to be wearing a black leather jacket and blue denim jeans. If anyone sees this woman or hears of her, or if anyone was a witness of the explosion that night, could you please contact p.w.w.t.p on the following number, 01234 567891.

Kelly McWilliams (13)
South Molton Community College, Devon

Anonymous!

I don't know who I am, I don't know why I'm here. I'm in the woods. It's dark, quiet and smells strongly of pine trees. Leaves and pine cones crunch under my feet as I walk. Nothing stirs in these woods, not even the leaves on the trees move as the breeze ripples through them.

I don't know where I am walking. I don't know where I am going but I don't know where I am so why stand still?

I am near the edge of the woods now, I can hear water crashing against rocks and running off the sand.

I am on a beach walking towards the sea, there are no boats, there are no animals, there's only me.

The beach starts disappearing under my feet, I'm in a room. It is quiet. A middle-aged woman is crying. There's a girl lying on a bed. She looks like me. I touch her face, it's cold, she's dead. The doctor starts talking.

'We are very sorry for your loss,' he says in a whisper to the woman. 'Her body could not keep fighting the cancer anymore.'

I didn't want to be there anymore. I wanted to be back on the beach by myself.

That's where I am now, all alone, by myself, just me.

Emily Page (14)
South Molton Community College, Devon

Bring On Arsenal

Ruud van Nistelrooy remains confident that Manchester United can beat Arsenal in the FA Cup semi-final despite Arsenal being unbeaten all season.

Nistelrooy has recently been told by striker partner Louis Saha that he is not as complete a player as Arsenal rival Thierry Henry. Ruud faces the critics on Saturday to show them why he is one of the world's best strikers. He will face a daunting task as he has not scored against Arsenal this season and hasn't been on top form lately.

Manager Sir Alex Ferguson says, 'Ruud has had a bad patch lately but has shown what he is about in training. I will keep him in the team as long as he is putting in the commitment and effort'. Arsenal will be favourites going into Saturday's clash as they are unbeaten but they have not beaten Man Utd all season. Gunners' captain Patrick Viera tells us why he thinks Arsenal are the best, 'At the moment and the way we're playing, we are nearly untouchable. Not Manchester United or even Real Madrid would be able to stop us'.

So with Arsenal going for the treble and Man Utd just the FA Cup, you can expect an enthralling match this Saturday.

Liam Craze (13)
South Molton Community College, Devon

A Day In The Life Of A Person On The Streets!

Yet again I wake to the same sunrise as I have seen every day for the last year. Anyone else on the Earth would love it, but not me, it's 'boring'. I see it every day.

I crawl out from under the bandstand where I spend most of my nights. I would say it was about 6.00 but I don't actually know. Saying that I don't even know what day it is.

I walk into town, and into the public toilets. I have a quick wash and put on the same dirty clothes I have worn for the last three weeks.

I move on, scouring the streets for food. There isn't any. I'll have to survive until tea, like I normally do.

The streets are filling up now with the hustle and bustle of people, it must be nearing nine o'clock.

I walk about the shops, looking for money and drinks. I eventually give up.

I take my normal place outside The Body Shop. I wait.

'Got any money for a cup of tea and breakfast?' I say to every passer-by.

Hardly anyone stops. If they do they throw 1 or 2p at me, not give, throw.

I stay there all day, just stopping when the odd cop comes by. I don't want to go to court again. I've been once and learnt from my mistake.

It's starting to get dark, better go and buy tea with the ten pounds I got today. Hopefully I'll have enough for breakfast tomorrow.

Sometimes I wish I was home with my dad, but I can't be, he's dead; all that is in his place is the wicked witch of the west: the horrible person he married.

Nikita Trainor-Roulstone (12)
South Molton Community College, Devon

Medusa And Luke Hercules In The Shooting Snakes

It was an ordinary day and I was walking down the road and I heard the most peculiar sound. It was coming from a dark hole in the ground, so I thought, *what the heck.* So I went to check it out, and the most ugliest revolting thing was there. I believed it had to be Dr Frostenstein's remake of Medusa, and believe me it looked like Medusa.

It as all slimy when I touched it and it growled, and then the snakes on its head, they just popped up and started snapping at me but these weren't like old Medusa's snakes no, these were magic snakes, enormous snakes, killing snakes, everything, you name it.

I was scared, I just hid under a table. Whilst I was under the table all I could think about was my great ancestor who killed Medusa 3,500 years ago: Hercules the great warrior. *Oh no*, I was running from the creature and then I saw a nice-looking spear, so I dashed for it to take Medusa down. I grabbed the spear, swiped it but Medusa knocked me down. I got back up and bit her leg and rammed it right through her heart. That was it: she turned to ashes. She was gone. I ran out of there and went back home.

I couldn't sleep that night because I was probably the most scared boy in the world. I said to myself, 'I went to the underworld, I survived and I'm never going there again.'

To be continued . . .

Adam Thorne (13)
South Molton Community College, Devon

The Answer

Never seems right getting up so early, but I suppose getting ready to go to court and fight off the lies that get thrown my way isn't so bad, well yes it is. Haven't been in court before. Well haven't been in the press before either, but like they say, *any publicity is good publicity.* Well that can be argued.

So sitting in the court everyone looking and all you can say is yes or no to every question and what you want to say is, *I didn't do it, stop blaming me*, but I suppose that isn't going to help me. OK, I'm sitting here waiting for my lawyer to have new evidence, but no, nothing, he just sits there. I suppose he doesn't care, I'm paying for him to sit there, whether I go down or not.

I don't know why in this world people can't tell the truth, I never did anything, but still get blamed for it. I think the person who did it framed me, but who is going to own up now? I'm on the stand not them, they can probably sit back and let me suffer and I suppose they are thinking, *well, it's nearly over! We did that well, who's next?*

Last day of questioning, some would say 'Judgement Day'. Well, I hope God's on my side today. My lawyer said he had new evidence which he presented to the court yesterday. I wasn't there yesterday, I don't know why, my lawyer said it was for the best, but I don't know.

So the judge asks for the answer, 'Guilty or not guilty?' The words shivered down my spine. Then came the answer . . . *Guilty.* The words stared me in the face and all I could think of was, *what happened yesterday?*

Anna Marie Cooke (14)
South Molton Community College, Devon

A Day In The Life Of A Soldier

It is my last day today. I'm going over the top and I feel helpless and terrible. My hands are shaking, my heart is pounding and I'm shivering. I can't do anything about it. I have to do what the generals say.

When I first heard about the war in 1939 I was over the moon with joy. Me and my friends joined up straight away. I was only young back then, nineteen I was. We got split up and they were all killed over the years, so I don't have any of them left with me.

My dad told me about the First Great War and he said it was totally different to what he had expected. He said, 'I thought it was going to be fun, you know, have a laugh with my friends while shooting the hell out of the Germans.' But I didn't believe him, why should I? He was old. He knew nothing. He said he was lucky that he was alive. I should have listened, but I didn't and now look where I am.

I'm basically just about to go and kill myself for no reason. I mean, how are we gaining land and progressing if we are all getting blown to bits by machine guns and .22 air rifles!

I thought that I would get to a high standard in the army, but I was wrong. I hate it here. The war ground is dead, there are just dead bodies everywhere and the stench is terrible. We are living in the mud. The landscape has been destroyed. The only animals left are the rats. They scavenge and eat everything that lies in their path.

I'm going now. Goodbye forever.

Brendan O'Boyle (14)
South Molton Community College, Devon

The Mysterious Monster

One day when I was walking to school, I met my best friend Zack outside Snows. As soon as Zack saw me he rushed over to me as quick as a hare and told me he saw something colossal, brown and hairy up near his house. I started laughing and thought he was joking. Then I realised he had a serious face and his voice sounded worried and frightened. I changed the subject quickly before he blabbered on even more.

All day I was thinking about what Zack said. I was horrified! Every lesson at school I was thinking about it and it was putting off my concentration throughout the lessons.

After school Zack came up to me and reminded me I was going over to his house. As we were walking back to his house he asked me, 'Do you wanna check out and see if we can find this monster thing?'

I paused for a moment and I knew if I didn't he would think I was a right coward, so I said, 'Yeah, alright.'

Both of us wrapped up warm and were getting ready to go. I was so scared and panicking already. Zack and I left at nine when it was dark and when no one was around. It was very damp and treacherous that night.

After about ten minutes Zack gave me a nudge and pointed over to a shed where we both saw this enormous, hairy thing, with its back facing us. I had never been so scared in my life. We slowly tiptoed over to the shed and crept up behind the monster. I was so close to running away, but we both wanted to find out what it was. So I gave it a poke and it suddenly clashed onto the floor and all it was, was a bulky, hairy rug.

Henry Payne (14)
South Molton Community College, Devon

The Filleigh Flyer

There was a shadow in the midnight sky while I heard a screeching noise. I thought it was a bird or a bat. I looked at the little house by the river, it flew into a barn or a shed next to it. I couldn't see what it was because it was dark.

My dog was running with his nose down, sniffing as he went up the wood. I knew he was on the scent of something and barked. He lifted up an arm and started to drag it towards me. I ran up the hill to this body and looked at it very carefully. There were teeth marks on its neck. It was a businessman because he was dressed in a suit and his briefcase was down the wood, in the swamp.

My dog ran off and started to bark, I heard the screeching noise again. The shadow was back. My dog howled then disappeared. I called his name over and over again, but there was endless silence. I walked on along the track through the dark, gloomy woods and kept calling his name. I heard a thump on the ground. To my astonishment there was my dog with wings and a huge beak, slouching, looking me in the eye. Before I could do anything about it he snatched at me with his beak, forcing me to the ground.

I woke up and discovered that I had wings and a huge beak like my dog. I don't know what happened but I am going to find a cure to turn my dog and I back to normal life.

Ben Warren (14)
South Molton Community College, Devon

The Daily Nightmare

A Twix wrapper floats across the road towards a shop entrance. I skip across, jumping from one white line to the other. I stumble up the pavement step and fall into the café window. A few sniggers are coming from the shop.

I lean over to pick up the wrapper. *Bang!* It's gone. Disappears under a familiar trainer, loose laces hanging over the side drenched in brown, murky water.

My heart skips a beat as I realise this is my daily nightmare. His trousers are halfway down his legs with snake eyes on each pocket which are covered up by his scruffy shirt hanging out; his tie halfway down his chest is sticking out of his collar.

I flinch from the sight of his face; all scared and battered, his eye looks as if it has bright purple make-up on. He had been in a fight - it is Reese from school!

All I can think about is running, I have practised sprinting at school before but I can only keep it up for about twenty seconds; still that seems the best option.

As I run I can feel Reese gaining on me, sweat dripping on my forehead and tears brimming in my eyes.

The alarm clock goes. I lie in bed half awake. I can barely open my eye from the fight. I manage to lift myself up. I put my trousers on; they have snake eyes on each pocket but you can hardly see them as they are covered up by my shirt, my new school shoes are now dyed brown from the murky water on the laces.

Harriet Bowman (13)
South Molton Community College, Devon

A Day In The Life Of Snail, The Horse

It was a light, cloudy evening when I arrived here at Calvert Trust. Today, (Saturday) I was ridden for the first time. It was Lizzy who rode me. When she brought me in from the field in the morning, she gave me a good brush (as I was pretty muddy). She came round with a white box full of leftover cabbage stumps from the kitchen. Lizzy wondered whether I would like it or not. It was actually quite tasty. During the day she had to get on with other things, like mucking out and leading.

After lunch she had to help with some lessons in the school. At about quarter to four she came over with Catherine and they tried a different rug on me, which fitted better, but Niki said that Bobby, April and June might fight with me, so I would be safer on my own.

At four o'clock Lizzy got me out, Catherine got Bobby and Niki got Duke. They tacked us up and took us in the school. When they were on, I was leading. To start we were just walking round, then I had to trot round. After, they did some cantering with me. I couldn't do much because I only had three shoes. Niki said I looked good and I thought Lizzy was a good rider.

When they were finished they put me out in the field and one by one put April, June, then Bobby in. They didn't seem to notice me. I had a good roll to finish the day and then went off to graze with Barley.

Lizzy Dallyn (13)
South Molton Community College, Devon

A Day In The Life Of An Elephant

This story is set in the centre of a dry, humid forest. It divulges us into the lifestyle of the spectacular, large, grey elephants.

Their day begins by awakening when the scorching red sun rises into a pale blue, cloudless sky. They begin by stretching their legs, waving their trunks and dozily murmuring.

After they're conscious they hunt for a scrumptious, nutritious breakfast like a stray cat rummages through an old tin dustbin.

When they've finished their first meal of the day, they plod to the river where they cool down from the boiling sun. On their way, they trample past the long, spiky-tipped grass and over the crispy, brown, dead leaves, which have fallen thousands of metres from the top of the skinny trees.

As they continue their strenuous trek the female herd notice an elegant middle-aged bull wandering around the trees. The group begin to wave their trunks and flick their ears back upon their shoulders as if they were humans playing with their hair flirtatiously.

When they eventually reach the animal pool, they dive in and cover themselves in soothing, cold water. Then suddenly, one elephant looks across the river to see the shadow of the handsome bull shimmering in the water.

The elephants then start to gradually leave the pool and eat a small lunch by grabbing some of the delicious grass and leaves which lay by the river.

The elephants then trek back to their base where they eat their supper and watch the sun slowly sink in the sky.

After that the elephant day is finally over and the herd lie down, shut their eyes, dream about the bull they saw earlier and wait for the sun to rise again tomorrow.

Suzanna Stanbury (12)
South Molton Community College, Devon

The Human Child

Marlee climbed up the cliff face, watching out for humans and other pandas. She had to get there. They might have found him already.

Finally she reached the cave. She crept round to the back and climbed up through the hole to the grotto. At first she couldn't see, but then she heard a cry. She went over and nuzzled his face with her nose. He seemed to like that. If the clan found him though, well she couldn't bear to think about it. A human child! In their midst! The elders would have a fit. Besides, when it grew up it would be a danger. How would it climb to the nests? The black and spotty cats would be smart enough to come looking for them. Especially if the human child was trying to reach the nest. He would have to go to a human nest place.

She gently picked him up and began the precarious climb to the bottom of the cliff, checking around her all the time.

At the bottom she secured him to her belly and began to swing towards the human nest place. It was not far thankfully, but she would have to wait for the dark time.

The clan were probably searching for her. She would be punished when she got back. She didn't care though. It was worth it to save the little child's life.

At dusk she silently padded through the nest homes. She saw the biggest one and decided to leave him there. The leader of their pack would look after him.

After gently laying him down, she ran off. Only pausing to look at him for one last time, then she was off . . .

Anita Eales (13)
South Molton Community College, Devon

The Vision

Share your world with us . . . please.

It was late in the evening when they heard it. The echo sounded through the trees as they rustled in the wind. The sound came deep from the woods in the hills. It rose from the peaks of the Carpathian mountains in the north. It drifted from the ice lands in the east. The sound waves covered everything, everywhere.

Men, women and children stopped to listen to the echoes that came from everywhere now. They listened in wonder to the brilliant music. And in the darkness, shooting stars flashed. Then, as if from nowhere, something happened that couldn't have been dreamt of, something that made terrified children leave their mothers' arms, walk alone and witness this casket of wonders.

Northern Lights traced the sky . . . if they really were the Northern Lights. Nobody cared that such a thing near the Carpathian mountains was impossible.

The lights danced dreamily and yet fiercely across the black sky. And still the singers continued, bringing dancing lights over the sky using only the power of their voices. Then suddenly, a vision came from these lights. It told people of the true bringers of peace, the Dream Catchers. It told of fortunes that could only come with the telling of the truth: The Masters of the Moonsong had arrived.

The wolves are here and they're here to stay. And with that, the vision ended, and the lights disappeared. Leaving only the wolves and a memory . . .

Help us survive.

Joanne Carnell (14)
South Molton Community College, Devon

The Cellar

'Whatever you do don't go into that cellar,' instructed Simon.

'I won't,' said Alison with an excited grin.

Simon disappeared down a small passage and left Alison standing next to the old, rusty cellar door. The door was overpowering and scary. Its hinges were brown with rust and the lock was the size of Alison's hands alone, no one had been in there before, no one was brave enough! With a huge push the lock screeched open, she had a peek through the small crack. It was as dark as the night sky. There were white, sparkling cobwebs twinkling like stars.

She crept in, suddenly the door closed trapping Alison inside. Hot air trickled down her neck like water. She turned, there was nothing there. Still, Alison looked around cautiously scanning the cellar for anything unusual. A blue flash of light caught her eye. She slowly walked towards it, her hands were shaking, half excitement and half fear. A blue lightning bolt shot into Alison's body. She started to fit, banging into the walls and knocking things off their shelves. This alerted Simon, he paced it back dropping his just bought shopping.

Simon heaved the door open and froze. Alison was spread out on the floor, her body ripped apart from the fitting. Something was calling to Simon, asking him to come in, he couldn't help it, he just started walking. As he did so the door slammed behind him again. Then the banging started once more.

Stephen Brook (14)
South Molton Community College, Devon

Murder Most Monstrous

A woman in her late twenties has been found dead in her own home. It is thought by police that she was murdered in the early hours on Friday 12th May.

Her body was discovered by police in her home at Knowstone, Devon yesterday.

She has not yet been identified as her body is almost unrecognisable due to the severity of the blows she received to the head and face. Despite this, doctors believe the cause of death to be strangulation and this should show in the autopsy which will be carried out today.

An investigation is of course being carried out to trace the murderer, or murderess as the case may be, but there are precious few trails for the police to follow.

Three witnesses have come forward but their information is thought to be insufficient and too vague to lay a solid foundation on for the investigation to follow.

The woman, who is believed to be in her late twenties, was found slumped on her kitchen floor. Contradictory to what appears to have been her murder scene, the investigators believe she may have been strangled in the sitting room and dragged into the adjoining kitchen.

Police were first alerted to the circumstance when a male, who still remains anonymous, telephoned them from what the police have traced to be a village telephone booth.

Police wish to speak to the caller as he is suspected of being related to the crime.

If anyone reading this has or knows of someone with knowledge or information on this disgusting abuse of human life then you are strongly urged and advised by the police to ring this number which will remain active until further official notice. The number is: 01249 569 220.

Maria Wheelan (14)
South Molton Community College, Devon

A Knight's Tale

My name is Max, a knight of the Round Table and this is my tale . . .

It has been years since the Round Table stood strong, twelve mighty warriors have slowly depleted to three. The kingdom of Balladale has enjoyed no peace for the last miserable decade, known as the years of the dragon. It hunts by night, ravaging all in its path. Many have tried and failed to slay this monster that killed my fellow warriors.

It became my duty to rid Balladale of this evil, but I could not do it alone. Two of the greatest warriors of the Round Table, William Axe Blood and Matthew of York, would fight by my side.

We travelled to Mort mountain for here was its lair, littered with rotting skeletons. We gulped and stepped inside, crouching for the roof of the cave was low. It was misty and the place stank of death. We reached the end and entered a vast, evil cavern.

Matthew stopped rigid, for facing us was a great red dragon, a flash of its terrible metre-long talons and William was dead before he hit the floor.

Matthew's sword swung and in return came a jet of flames that scorched my shoulders. I fell in agony while Matthew sent a fearsome blow into the leg of the dragon. It roared and with my last ounce of energy I hurled my sword into its unscaled underbelly. It fell with an almighty crash to the floor and lay still. Balladale was saved.

Matthew Coxon (12)
South Molton Community College, Devon

Hercules And Hades

Hercules was the son of Zeus, who was head of the Greek gods. He was a legend throughout Greece as he had stopped Hades (who was Lord of the Underworld) from freeing the dead.

Hercules was worried though for his father, Zeus, was dying of Belulabongolabambulafruitytuty syndrome (or Belututy syndrome for short) and the disease could only be cured by the petals of the cabdab plant. The trouble was though, that this plant was only found in a place called London, England.

That day he sailed there with the best ship in Greece because his winged horse, Pegasus, was tired from flying to Australia and back only two days before.

They sailed down the river and into the rainforest. He sailed through there with ease, brushing aside vines. He then jumped off the boat and walked into a clearing where a man was drinking the blood of a unicorn, the creature that Hercules loves the most. Without thinking he ran up to him and swung his sword at him but it just sliced through him. The man turned, it was Hades. He had escaped from the Chamber of the Dead in the Underworld. A fierce grin came across his face and then Hercules remembered the cabdab plant. *One petal will save you, two petals will kill you.* He looked to his left, there it was.

Hades was still just standing there, grinning. Hercules rolled to the flower picked two petals off and pushed them into Hades' stomach. He disappeared in a puff of smoke. Hercules looked at the flower, there was one petal left, enough to cure his father . . .

Simon Lockyer (13)
South Molton Community College, Devon

The Illustrated Mum

(An additional chapter written by me as inspired by Jacqueline Wilson)

Our social worker, drove us back to Aunt Jane's house, after our little visit to see Mum. I still felt mean about getting Mum into hospital, because I know how much she despises hospitals, but what was I supposed to do? I had no Star, because she was at her dad's and Mum paints herself with white gloss paint, she wasn't at all well.

Although today Mum looked a great deal calmer than usual, the hospital seems to be doing good to her. Mum can't help the way she is, she just has a problem, I was surprised she acted calm today considering she has funny turns. She is still the best mum in the world!

When Star and I were living together, Mum always tried to play silly games, or she would bake treats, she'd tried so hard, but Star never joined in, she always said she was too old for childish games or else insisted that she had heaps of homework to do; they were silly excuses.

It's weird, when I was little it was always Mum and Star, they were the colourful ones, they were always together like sisters and I just followed them. But now . . . Star can't stick Mum, she certainly showed it in the car, saying hateful things about Mum and mentioning that Mum was crazy. That was the final straw, I burst into angry sobs; we had never called Mum crazy, Star also said she wasn't a fit mother.

But it will end happily, I know it. Mum, Star and me! Together, forever!

Chrstina Hayes (13)
South Molton Community College, Devon

The Shadowed Serpent

One day a group of great white sharks were swarming off the bay of California. Suddenly a scream of *'Help'* was echoed from the nearby beach. A little girl was screaming, 'Snake, snake,' which she had seen in the distance in the ocean. It was heading for the sharks; the beach was in chaos, full of shocked, innocent civilians.

The snake was 18ft long with red, drawling eyes and yellow, daring fangs and it was heading head-on with the sharks. It was hissing and spitting with its head just below the surface. The sharks were too slow, six of them had spotted the snake earlier and had swum away, but the other two, well . . . were just doomed. The serpent had tasted blood once again; the blood had coated the sea with red gore.

The news of this attack was reported to the 'Sea Water Marine Safety', the report had said that a giant snake had attacked one or more sharks and was out to kill again! So the SWMS were on the look-out for this snake; they were loaded with harpoon guns and other artillery.

The SWMS were searching for the beast along where it had last been spotted, with their rescue boat, when a crash of ocean explosion just roared up behind them. The serpent had just taken a massive mouthful out of the side of the lifeboat. No more was heard of the lifeboat crew; people still say they drowned, some people say the serpent got them.

But still the shadowed serpent lurks on the seabed of the ocean.

James Tapp (12)
South Molton Community College, Devon

The Sleepover

It all started at that fateful sleepover. Emily came round and, as usual, we started to get a bit bored. We, I mean I, decided that we should go up and explore the attic. Emily agreed at first, but as we got closer to the pull-down stairs, she began to get nervous.

Once I had finally persuaded her, we made out way up into the darkness. I pulled out the torch that was in my pocket. It was only then that I realised that my annoying little sister Chloe had followed us up there. Just as I was about to tell her to go away, she whispered the word, 'Mum,' and then I remembered Chloe could go and tell Mum that we were up there, and we wouldn't be able to look around! She stayed. Big mistake!

'Hey, look at this!' Chloe yelled out to us. She found a book. I should have realised what would happen when we opened it. Anyway, when Chloe opened this book, things started coming out of it, hands. They grabbed me and Emily and dragged us into the book.

It took us to a graveyard. Well, it did eventually! Everything seemed normal, until we saw my mum. She didn't know who I was! She threw us onto the street. There was a flash of light. We were in the graveyard. We had to hunt around a bit, but we finally found a book similar to the other one. We opened it and found ourselves back in my attic. We thought everything was back to normal. How wrong could we be?

Emma Wilson (12)
South Molton Community College, Devon

Myths and Legends

A long time ago there was a young slave girl, part of the workforce for the construction of the forest city of Jamillia. This girl was a hard worker loved by all who knew her, but she had one dark secret, her hidden love for her master, the ruler of this new city and land, but as she was a slave she could never openly admit her love to anybody except one.

When she was very young she found all alone a young female bear cub. As they grew they formed a bond so tight that they could know what the other was thinking and in this way could share everything they felt and each would sacrifice itself for the other.

The girl loved her master and was grief-stricken as he would never even notice her. For twenty years she lived this way until, at the age of 40, she died, old before her time, aged by her grief. But as she died her spirit flew to its bond mate, Jonqui the bear. For one season they lived as one living life one moment at a time, not looking to the days ahead.

Until one day the bear visited the girl's grave and tore it open, gently lifted the girl's body out of the ground. Her spirit slammed into her old body forcing it into life, her second life where no one knew her as a slave. From here she proceeded into the new city to search for her lost love, but she failed as she was too much like a bear and was killed for being mad.

And so, to this day lives an ancient bear searching for its bond mate, not resting till it does.

Craig Milner (14)
Torquay Boys' Grammar School, Devon

My Myth

The soft trickle of the sea echoed around the trees as the wind coolly swayed the fragile plants. Frequently, the sand would be lifted and form layers over the moist moss. The sheer heat of the sun darkened the bark and reflected off the sea to form a beautiful aqua colour.

However, there lies a dark secret that has been kept for millions of years. The villagers of a nearby island are the only ones to know and never speak of it. They'd be arrested if they did. Nobody dares to go there. In the cluster of trees there is a parting which forms a perfect circle. A shallow ditch is situated in the centre. It is black.

Thirty years ago, a psychotic assassin roamed the streets of Bodmin. He increased his murder toll to seventeen when he brutally slashed a young girl. This young girl was six years old and attended the local primary school. At the more recent summer fair, she had done a clairvoyant a favour and was promised an unknown repayment. When she died, the favour had not been repaid. She lost her body but her soul remains - in the ditch. She is bitter and desperately seeks revenge on the human race, but she can only be released when she is spotted by a living person. It is said, if she is set free, she has the power to destroy anything she wants. The villagers will never tell, but will never forget.

Alex Molyneux (14)
Torquay Boys' Grammar School, Devon

Night And Day

Zulon was the god of the sun. The energy from the sun gave Zulon his power. The sun also stored the world's energy. The person controlling the sun was controller of the world. Without it, the Earth would be a dark and misty place.

In the deep, dark, hellish realm of Zion, the Underworld, was Kumon. He didn't like Zulon controlling the Earth and so he wanted to make the world dark and evil. He wanted to have the world for himself. He had a plot to capture Zulon's son Kia. In return for Kia, Zulon would have to swap the sun for his beloved son. His love for his son was dear, but Zulon didn't like this so he set out to destroy Kumon and regain his son.

On the way down to Zion, Zulon was attacked by Kumon's loyal servants. Kumon then had the chance to grab the sun. He took the sun to the deepest, darkest part of the Underworld. Zulon had had enough so he went to redeem the sun and his son.

At the entrance to the Underworld Kumon and Zulon battled, but Kumon won because Zulon had no energy source. At his father's death Kia awoke from his deep trance. He tried to defeat Kumon, but he was weak. Both near death, the selfish Kumon spoke, he said Kia could have the sun, but only for twelve hours so they could regain their health. So then, once strong enough, the battle for eternal darkness or eternal light continued.

Luke Fisher (13)
Torquay Boys' Grammar School, Devon

How Italy Was Formed (My Legend)

A long time ago in Europe there was an epic battle between the war god, Ares and a terrible monster that had been attacking and causing trouble for the gods for many years. The monster was huge and said to have spawned from the deepest place in the Earth. It had legs of a man, the body of a leopard and the head of a fire-breathing dragon. The gods feared this terrible beast, but one day Ares had had enough of the torment that the monster had caused and decided to try and kill it.

The epic battle took place in Europe, and the two enemies fought ferociously for many days and blood from each warrior was spilt all over Europe.

It looked as if Ares was going to lose until one of his swipes with his sword hit the monster and the monster's leg fell off and landed at the edge of Europe just resting on France. Ares then took advantage of the monster's pain and thrust his sword into the monster's chest, blood spilled everywhere. The monster's limp body fell to the floor. Ares then dragged the body into the ocean, but Ares forgot about the leg of the monster and after a time it started to become part of Europe. Ares then sprinkled dirt onto the leg of the monster so that no living man would ever see the hideousness of it.

That leg became the country we call Italy.

Tom Cartwright (14)
Torquay Boys' Grammar School, Devon

The Story Of The Sun And The Moon

Once upon a time, long, long ago, the world was in harmony and the sun always shone. There was light everywhere and the sky was ruled by the sun and the world was full of good.

This was all to change, in the far corners of the air realm the dark lord, the moon, and his followers, the stars, were beginning to stir and were growing stronger with every passing minute. Long ago the sun had banished them from the central skies by a great miracle of light.

When the sun heard of this uprising he was shocked and sent for his elite flame warriors to build him a fort from the clouds, bigger and stronger than any other to repel the dark forces for good. The sun was almost too late as unbeknown to him, at the exact moment the fort was finished the moon had gathered his forces and begun his march to the central skies to claim his rule.

The dark forces reached the great fort of light after five long days and set siege to it. It was a long and terrible battle that was fought between the blinding flames and the cold stars with horrific death and superb bravery, but in the end the fort was destroyed along with the flames and the stars and all that was left was the sun and the moon. The two became locked in an epic battle to win or lose all, they fought like beasts but in the end neither had prevailed, but both were bruised and battered.

Suddenly there was a phenomenon, the sky went light and there was a piercing noise and both were put into an enchanted sleep. The sleep was to make the sun wake for half a day and there would be light, then the sun would sleep again and the moon would wake to bring darkness. That has been the way of the realm of the sky until this very day.

Tom Haysom (14)
Torquay Boys' Grammar School, Devon

The Legend Of Tizaz

Tizaz was the uncle of the universe. He was the direct brother to the king of the Underworld, Hades. Tizaz had it in his blood to be ferocious and very cruel. He would steal, kill, destroy; whatever it took to bring general pain and suffering to the entire universe and its people.

He had ten raven-like heads, with giant talons as big as twenty men. His eyes were evil with red blood from everyone he had slaughtered and they would flicker now and again. His body was a jumbled mess of guts and slime. At the mere sight of Tizaz everything fled, there was not one being that could stand up against this creature of hell.

Tizaz had no birthplace; he was created in the fiery pits of Hell in a parallel universe. He was given wings so he could fly and join in unity with his brother and torment the world that existed, before death.

Tizaz had one problem; this was Agutez his maker. Agutez had been betrayed and wanted revenge. He had been building up with rage and soon, he could not hold it in any longer. They fought. At first Agutez threw meteors, but Tizaz was impervious to them. Tizaz rebounded his attack with a wave of fire. Agutez was thrown across the battlefield. Suddenly Agutez thought of his betrayal and burst out with fury. He shouted like nothing had ever sounded before. Tizaz was swept off his feet and into the air. He landed onto Agutez's spiked tail. His stomach was ripped apart and Agutez tore the wounded beast limb by limb and separated his parts and placed them in the corners of the universe. Tizaz was never seen again and the universe was no longer in threat.

James Hanbury (14)
Torquay Boys' Grammar School, Devon

The Myth Of Benland

In Benland, when children get to the age of six, it is traditional for their parents to tell them the myth of Benland. It goes a little something like this:

Once upon a time in Mexico there was a giant called Gullivernio the Great. He lived on the island of Lilipundos, just off Mexico.

One day, a huge storm hit the island and the locals of Lilipundos were doomed. The island was sinking. The local mouse, Quickly Gonzalez was running around like a headless chicken. Then it struck Gullivernio. He could take the locals of Lilipundos over the ocean to the uninhabited, paradise island of Benland.

So Gullivernio rounded up all the locals of Lilipundos (except for the taxman, Senõr Cato) and put them in a giant-sized El Sainsbriano carrier bag and waded across the ocean to Benland.

The new locals of Benland were ecstatic and lived like kings. Sadly, when Gullivernio dropped the people off at Benland, he was eaten by a huge albino whale. The locals named the beach on the west coast of the island The Beach of Gullivernio, in memory of the giant and they named the shore on the east coast of the island Albino Whale Shore, because that is where the huge albino whale ate Gullivernio.

Ben Kadory (13)
Torquay Boys' Grammar School, Devon

An Old Myth Of Wisdom And Time

Long ago in the ancient land of Greece, there was a conflict. This conflict was between two gods, the might Poseidon of the oceans and the god Titan who was the strongest hand-to-hand fighter in the land of Greece. Titan was a ruler of the islands of Chausia, where he had been king for a whole 456 years. He was not favoured at all by his people, but he was renowned for defending his islands and gaining new land for them to expand, but he was cruel and he was hated by many gods around for his pitch-black skin and his evil look.

Poseidon and Titan were in another fight and this was the biggest one they had had in years. Titan wanted more land for his islands from the sea, which he would pound up from the seabed with his almighty fists. Poseidon would have none of it and each time Titan tried to gain new land Poseidon would flood it back into the sea. Titan would complain to Poseidon that he had as much sea as he wanted and that he would not miss a few acres gone from his oceans.

One day the islanders thought of a trick, they said to Titan that Poseidon dropped by and wanted a chat about the arrangement of giving Titan some land. Poseidon would be waiting in the back of the island of Zedos.

When Poseidon came by they said what they said to Titan and they said to Poseidon that he could ambush Titan and capture him for good, chaining him down to the bottom of the ocean for good with the powers of his oceans.

Poseidon did just this and Titan was trapped for good. The people of the Chausia islands were happy and every time Titan breathed for air under the ocean, it made waves on the shores on every coast of Greece.

Mark Foale (14)
Torquay Boys' Grammar School, Devon

Why The Sun Comes Up In The Morning And Goes Away At Night

Once upon a time the people in New Guinea believed that the sun was owned by a young man who kept it in a dish. He had inherited the sun from his father, an extremely powerful god. Now, the young man lived with his sister who prepared his meals and generally looked after him. When she married, her husband became jealous of him. He bullied him and gave him stones to eat instead of proper food. The young man decided to leave and go elsewhere

Taking the sun with him he headed off in his canoe towards the east. There he landed on a beach and fell asleep. He was woken by a group of young women who brought him food and gifts. They welcomed him warmly and made him king of their island because he was the only man and had brought the sunshine with him.

Meanwhile, back in his home village it was forever night. The people found they could grow no food in the darkness so soon they found themselves starving to death. The young man's sister set off in search of her brother, the owner of the sun.

She travelled far and wide and eventually saw a stream of light in the east. At long last she landed on the island where her brother was king and begged him to come back home with her and bring the sun with him. The young man agreed and put the sun in his sister's boat and together they travelled westwards. When the people saw the sun's light shining down on them and their island they were able to grow their food once more.

However, the owner of the sun did not remain on his home island, but sailed away to the island where he was king. Nevertheless, he promised to return every morning and he has kept his promise to this day.

William Pike (14)
Torquay Boys' Grammar School, Devon

The Monkey's Paw - 10 Years Later

Mr Carter had inherited the magical monkey's paw - cursed by an old Indian vizier. It had strange and terrible powers to punish those who meddled with fate. Mr Carter's family had heard many tales of its destructive powers and were well aware of its dangers. Despite this, his son John could not resist showing it to his friends, of whom I was one.

'And so whatever you do, don't touch the paw,' John called out to me as he went upstairs to bed.

For a minute or two I just stared at it wondering what I should do, should I wish or should I not? If I could just be specific enough with the wish and not ask for much, a new bike or something, what could happen? I mean, surely no deaths or anything like that! On the other hand, I had heard what it had done before and knew it was not worth the risk.

Suddenly, to remove the temptation, I threw the paw onto the fire (just like the general John had told me about, had done all those years ago). Colourful sparks erupted as the paw flew out of the fire and landed on the table where it had been lying before.

In a state of shock, I picked up the paw and started to think of a wish. What did I really want? Wishing for money would be too risky, but suddenly it came to me, a trumpet. So I wished. I rubbed the paw and said out loud, 'I want a trumpet.'

Nothing happened - the paw didn't move. Disappointed I put it back on the table and went to my room.

Next morning, Mrs Carter woke me. She was white as a sheet. 'What is it?' I asked. The reply was shocking. John was dead!

A few days later, a parcel arrived in the post addressed to me. Thinking nothing of it, I opened it to discover a black case labelled 'Barnaby's Musical Instruments'. Slowly I opened the case and to my horror, it contained a trumpet with a note from John's mother saying that he would have wanted me to have it.

William Dewing (14)
Torquay Boys' Grammar School, Devon

Myths And Legends

Once upon a time, in a nearby town there lived an old man. This old man had a very strict routine. Every day he would go to church at 12.00 and then, after the service, would return home straightaway. One day he decided to walk home via the shops. As he walked past the shops, he saw the local police station. He remembered his days in the police force and just took a moment to remind himself of all the good memories that he had. Once he had got everything that he needed from the shops, he decided to walk home through the beautiful country lane. Once again this was not something he did very often, but he thought that it was time for a change.

As he walked through the lanes, he stopped now and again to look at the corn fields and buzzards flying swiftly through the air. He thought that it was beautiful and decided from that day forward he would walk home through those lanes. As he carried on through the lanes, he came to a corner. As he turned the corner, to start on the path which led to his house, a car came flying down the lane. The old man did not have time to move and the car ran him over. The man was killed instantly on the spot.

After this, speed bumps were put into the roads. They were used to reduce people's speed and reduce death. These were called sleeping policemen after the old man who was killed. They were and are very successful.

Matthew Foulger (13)
Torquay Boys' Grammar School, Devon

The Myth Of The Growing Tree

Over 3,000 million years ago, an octopus was born into the world; a world of raging seas and barren deserts. However this was no ordinary octopus. This octopus had nine tentacles, and was named Nonopus. All the other octupuses made fun of Nonopus, as he was unusual and stood out from the crowd. Nonopus was so annoyed and frustrated by this, that he ran away from the others and hid by digging under the seabed, he burrowed and burrowed until he was well away from the other horrible octopuses.

He fed on bugs and worms deep under the Earth's surface as he dug and dug. He dug so hard that his tentacles grew hard and strong to adapt to the endless digging. He even grew more arms to help propel himself through the dense material.

However, Nonopus slowly grew weak. He slowed from the dense soil that surrounded him until eventually he came to a halt. Nonopus was stuck. He tried to push himself up but to no avail. One push would perhaps push him up a fraction of a centimetre. He was going to be there for a long time.

In fact, he's still there now, slowly pushing upwards in the hope of shelter and freedom. He's so close to the surface now, that with every push, one of his arms reaches out of the surface and stretches out in triumph. First, just a fingertip. And then it grows until his whole arm is showing. This arm is what we today, 3,000 million years later, call a tree.

Andrew Reeve (13)
Torquay Boys' Grammar School, Devon

My Myth Or Legend

There once was an island called Icilla. In that island there is a village called Silda. In this village lived a giant who helped the people of Silda to live a safer life.

One day the people of Silda woke up to what seemed to be an earthquake, but was it? The giant looked out of his window and saw another giant from the land of Rilla trying to ruin the village. So, he stomped out of his house to save the village.

When he was only 50 metres away from the other giant, he shouted to him, 'What are you doing?' but the other giant just kept stamping on the village. As a result, the giant started to fight the other giant to save the village, but the other giant saw him and ran to the volcano which created the island.

On the volcano, an epic battle started. Eventually, after some time, the giant pushed the other giant into the volcano which led to the other giant being pushed down the volcano to a dangerous death.

After this the giant was seen as a hero or the protector of the island Icilla. No one ever came to Icilla trying to overcome the giant because every monster or person was too scared to try and beat the giant.

The giant eventually did die but now he is remembered by a statue and he is buried deep under the sea.

Ben Slater (13)
Torquay Boys' Grammar School, Devon

Wings Of Dragonia

I watched an easterly sun drown in amber fire, as it sank below the crest of ancient hills. I watched as I and my species always do; eternal, sentient and forever blessed. Radiant rainbow-coloured light, as bright as the heavens, caressed the grasslands around me like a loving mother does her young. I am a dragon, not a stereotypical dragon as mortals tend to indulge themselves in, but a sovereign entity, a guardian of all worlds; immortal, powerful, but serene and gentle also.

The vagrant wind brushed lightly against my smooth, red scales. It felt good, and I let it flow around my body. I am two metres three centimetres tall, using the mortal measuring units, which is about ten below average dragonic height. I relate this from Dragonia, sacred realm of dragons and sovereign entities, which exists in a parallel universe if you see it like that. Basically it exists in an area of the cosmos which is unable to be accessed through any ordinary means; you need to use portals and teleportation in order to reach it.

Dragonia itself is beautiful beyond measure, and we sovereign protect it with all our powers. When I refer to the sovereign, I mean us dragons, phoenixes and Dragonian foxes. We are classed as sovereign as we are the strongest of all species, but equal also, and although we have scales, we are not reptiles, as phoenixes aren't birds and Dragonian foxes aren't mammals. We are sovereign, we can interbreed at will.

Tom Voelske (14)
Torquay Boys' Grammar School, Devon

Chuan's Mistake

Two hundred thousand years ago lived the great Chinese ruler, Chuan Chao. He had control of the whole of China, but things were not going well. Massive parts of the country had rebelled and they did not want Chuan as leader, he needed to take control.

The Chinese leader decided to change himself, he gave himself new powers. He made anyone he touched turn into dust and he changed himself into a giant with claws the size of men.

With these powers, he ruled the whole of China without any problems. He built himself a huge palace with a thousand servants; he had everything he had ever dreamt of, apart from one thing, a friend.

So Chuan decided to make a friend. His friend would be just as powerful as him and could help him rule. Chuan created a ferocious beast and named him Wai Lok.

The two were getting on really well. Chuan now had, truly, everything he wanted. They decided that they could rule the country together equally, but Wai Lok did not agree, he wanted more.

'I am much more powerful than you, I deserve more,' he roared.

'No you're not, I created you, you worthless piece of waste,' replied Chuan.

The dispute went on until it got out of hand and became physical.

The two giants battled into the great city of Yin. The giants fought and fought until they could fight no more. Chuan and Wai Lok collapsed in a heap and did not survive.

Tom Whittle (14)
Torquay Boys' Grammar School, Devon

The Hole Of Eternity

There once was an old lady who had no relatives, no friends, not even a pet. She lived on her own in a small but comfortable burrow. She wasn't an animal though. She was small, frail and had a very skinny body. No wonder she was so skinny, she had lived on oak tree root stew for the past 168 years.

Her burrow was a special burrow, it was thought to have special powers, powers that could make you live forever. The entrance to the burrow was very small and was covered by a large slab of granite which was mined locally. The lady was called Millie and she would always wear a pair of sunglasses and a baseball cap, trying to keep up with what she thought was today's fashion. She wore this for another reason, if any part of her bare skin was to make contact with a ray of sunlight she would die. The Hole of Eternity was real. The hole could keep you alive for hundreds of years.

One hot summer's day, a set of diggers rolled up Old Oak Hill and started to flatten it, taking parts of the hill away bit by bit. When they found her, she was dead.

Tom Lakeman (13)
Torquay Boys' Grammar School, Devon

A Day In The Life Of Sir Toby

At 7 o'clock this morning I woke up with a bit of a hangover and found I couldn't remember what had happened the night before. So I went down to breakfast. I had the usual, 3 eggs, 4 rashers of bacon, 2 slices of toast and a pint of lager. Umm delicious.

At 8 o'clock, me and Sir Andy sat down with a pint and tried to remember what had happened the night before and I fell asleep on the sofa. When I finally awoke, Malvolio was standing over me and it suddenly hit me what we had done the night before, we had had a party. Malvolio started shouting at me but as I was only half awake, all I heard was food and drink, I immediately thought of lamb chops and I started drooling. Malvolio stormed off in disgust.

After he had left, I went looking for my sheep, Sir Andy. After I found him, we decided to go for a ride in my carriage and it was during our ride that suddenly we hit a bump and my lager fell out of my hand. I was outraged. So I opened my mini bar and got another one out.

About 3 o'clock I saw Malvolio crossing the lane so I took the reins from the driver, I had to pay Malvolio back for shouting at me earlier in the morning. The police always said never to drink and drive but this was too good a chance to miss. I made the horses brake for the full impact and I hit him. It was a direct hit, I didn't want to kill him but half of me did. But he didn't die, he just broke both of his legs.

At 6 o'clock I didn't have any guilt so I invited Sir Andy and Feste and we partied. Oh what a night.

Matt West (13)
Torquay Boys' Grammar School, Devon

Stakeout

He had been told to wait on the street corner, underneath the bridge. It was raining hard. His fingers were freezing from the cold, metal handle of the large, metal briefcase in his hand. He wore a large black trench coat over the top of his Armani suit.

After a few minutes, a black Mercedes with blacked-out windows pulled slowly around the corner and stopped. This man also wore a trench coat but with a small leather hat that shaded his face from the nearby street light.

A chunky-looking bouncer stepped out of the car and held an umbrella over the new man.

'I see you've got the money,' said the second man as he reached into the car to retrieve a similar briefcase.

'I see you're under arrest,' replied the first man.

'What?' The second man's strong American-Italian accent broke for a second out of fear.

Suddenly the first man, AKA Lieutenant John Forsham of LAPD whipped his foot around into the bouncer's neck, a pressure point. His head flopped to his shoulders and he fell against the car, causing the car alarm to go off.

Forsham and the second man both pulled out guns and pointed them at each other's heads. The loud car alarm was pounding into their heads, they couldn't think. A blowing sound came from across the road. A couple of seconds later, the second man was on the floor, the tranquilliser's red flight was sticking from his neck. Forsham's team had done it!

Dan Haslam (13)
Torquay Boys' Grammar School, Devon

Canadian Secrets

The cold reaches through my whole wardrobe. No, I'm not *in* the wardrobe. I'm on a government expedition to Canada, to prove the yeti exists. No one knows we're here. No one will know if we die. I'm here with my fiancé and his colleagues. I guess I'm not really like them; I'm Canadian, they're English, but it's cold, even to me.

We're going on patrol. It's started to snow. I can't see anything. I think we've been separated. I'm cold. I'm also getting messages from my bladder. The snow is a blanket, suffocating and blinding. 'I'm on a mountain, lost, cold and scared,' I say aloud, 'isn't this fun?' It all goes dark.

I'm in a cave. It's dark but light is filtering in. There's a face above me. Deep, intense brown eyes. Red hair. This isn't human. This is the Sasquatch. There's an arm next to me. Arms shouldn't bend that way. Glad it's not mine. It's my fiancé and his friends. They're talking quietly. I know what they're talking about.

They want to sell it on the black market. I look at the yeti. Its eyes are sad. And something else - anger? Angry they're here? Angry they want to imprison it? This has happened before. No one will know if they die. Except me.

My secret.

My Canadian secret.

Kenya Rolfe (11)
Tower House Private School, Devon